for another Elizabeth

Chapter One

"She has *what?*" Thomas, Marquis of Worthington, paused in pacing his London study to slam a fist on the ornately carved table. Since he was but lately recovered from a wound suffered in the Peninsular War, the pain that jolted down his arm brought a ready curse to his lips.

James Mitchell looked up from the figures he was adding and surveyed his employer. "I'm afraid it's true, milord. She's already bought a building on Piccadilly Street and she says she plans to turn it into a museum. Wants to rival Bullock's Egyptian Hall."

The marquis scowled and took another turn around the room, the resounding heels of his shining Hessians echoing his agitation and setting the delicate Sèvres porcelain to quivering. "Folly!" he exclaimed. "Sheer folly."

He stopped and faced his steward. Confound it, why must the fellow remain so calm? The marquis was feeling the effects of the hereditary Worthington temper and yearning for the chance to yell at someone.

This damned shoulder had made him as irritable as an infantryman with too tight boots. And this abominable London summer had tempers soaring with the temperature.

But, he reminded himself, he was a fair-minded man. He did not browbeat those who worked for him, especially those as good at their work as James Mitchell. "And what has the *ton* to say about this bit of stupidity?" he inquired, easing himself into a delicate lyre-backed chair.

Mitchell permitted himself a small smile. "I believe, milord, that they are much of the same opinion as you. Lady Elizabeth's new scientific museum has already been nicknamed Farrington's Folly."

"I might have known." Worthington leaned back and stretched his long legs. "She was always making trouble," he remarked. "She's that sort."

Mitchell put down his quill. "I have heard that said about her. I have also heard that she's considered a reigning beauty."

The marquis looked up in surprise. "Impossible! That scrawny carrot-top a beauty?"

Mitchell coughed discreetly. "Might I suggest, milord, that with you away at war, it has been some years since you've actually seen the lady?"

Worthington considered this. "Yes. 'Spose it has. Just before I went off to Eton, I think. The little devil threw a shrunken head at me! Hit me in the stomach, as I recall."

Mitchell struggled to suppress his laughter and failed. Worthington, his good humor restored, grinned. "Go ahead, man — laugh. It does sound amusing."

Absently he rubbed his aching shoulder. "Let me tell you about the lady. The first time I met her she pushed me into her father's fish pond."

"Milord!"

"It's true." His lordship's grin widened. "She's a menace to mankind. Let's see." He ticked items off on his fingers. "She knocked me out of the apple tree. Made my pony run away. Turned my pet frogs loose into the pond. Put a spider in my bread and butter. And that was just for starters."

By now Mitchell was shaking his head in disbelief. "How old was she then?"

"Probably about six. She made my summers quite exciting, I can tell you. Till I grew too old for such playmates."

Mitchell smiled. "I guess what they say about her must be true."

Worthington frowned, his dark eyes narrowing. "And what do they say?"

"That she must always have her own way. That she regards no opinion but her own."

"They're right about that." Worthington made a moue of distaste. "And of course my father had to make me swear to look out for her. A good man, my father, but a trifle too kindhearted."

Since the present marquis was known far and wide for numerous charitable acts which he tried in vain to keep secret, Mitchell could only nod.

"I'm afraid, milord, that looking out for her is all you *can* do. For some strange reason the late Lord Farrington left everything in her control."

Worthington scowled. "The earl was a strange man. Doted on that little minx. Had some other peculiar likings, too. That cabinet of curiosities he kept was —" He smiled ruefully. "The room *was* exciting, full of strange, exotic things. And dash it, man, I have to admit it, I played with the shrunken heads, too."

His scowl returned. "But I'm a man now. I've outgrown such childish things. And I've got to look out for her."

He sighed. "Her father should have made me her legal guardian. No woman knows enough to handle her own wealth. The fortune hunters will be after her in droves."

Mitchell chuckled. "From what I hear, the lady has already dispatched several of those. With admirable spirit."

Worthington shook his head. "Then she'll squander her money. On gowns. Or bonnets. Or shrunken heads. Who knows?"

In the drawing room of her house off Grosvenor Square, Elizabeth, Lady Farrington, was at that moment examining her latest acquisition in the shrunken head line.

"It's the most amazing thing," she said to her old nurse. "The way everything shrinks in proportion."

" 'Tis not amazing," whined Nanny, her seamed face wrinkling in dismay. " 'Tis disgusting, that's what it is! A grown woman of four-and-twenty playing with the remains of a human like that!"

Elizabeth shrugged. "Oh, Nanny, don't be so — so — this is a scientific item."

"Scientific, indeed!" snorted Nanny. "Don't see as how preserving a man's head is scientific at all. 'Tis barbarous, that's what it is."

"Of course it is scientific," Elizabeth insisted, with the confidence that comes from never having been proven wrong. "Think of what they must know about preserving."

"Don't want to think of it." Nanny shuddered and pulled her shawl closer. "I just don't know," she murmured to no one in particular. "I did all I could. I raised her in the right ways. But it didn't take. I've failed, oh Lord!" She moaned and cast her eyes heavenward. "I've failed in my bounden duty."

Elizabeth put the shrunken head back in its box and crossed the room to confront the old woman. "Nonsense, Nanny. You're the best nurse a little girl ever had." She smiled. "But I'm not a little girl any more. I'm a woman now."

Nanny nodded. "That you are. And you should be out looking for a husband. Not for five-legged goats and two-headed chickens." Her voice rose. "It ain't decent, it ain't. A young woman of your station, gallivanting around the countryside, hanging about with such riffraff."

Elizabeth swallowed a smile. "Now, Nanny. Madame Nuranova isn't riffraff. Why, she's a queen."

Nanny drew herself up. "And I'm the king's daughter myself," she said with a decided sniff. "Queen, indeed! She's one of them gypsies, pure and simple. Ain't no real queen going to be with them gypsies. They're — they're — well, it just ain't right."

Elizabeth allowed herself a smile. Dear old Nanny, always complaining. "Madame Nuranova can tell the future. Don't you want to know what the future holds?"

"Shades of the devil," Nanny whispered. "What crazy thing'll you be doing next?" She heaved a tremulous sigh. "It ain't Christian to be poking around with such things." She shuddered. " 'Tis evil to be trying to know what's to come. The good Lord keeps the knowledge of the future from us for our own good."

Elizabeth nodded. Nanny was probably right. She herself would not have wanted to know ahead of time about Papa's death — or the other calamities human flesh was heir to. But it would really be nice to know that a husband was waiting, somewhere, there in her future.

"You know, Nanny, that I have tried to find a husband. Look how many men have courted me."

"But you didn't marry a one!" Nanny cried.

Elizabeth chuckled. "That's because I need a man for only one reason — for love. Papa left me well off, you know. I don't need a man to protect me . . . or support me." She sobered. "Or waste my substance."

Nanny frowned. "It just ain't natural. A

woman needs a husband and little ones."

Elizabeth patted her arm. "I know, Nanny. And I do wish to marry. But it must be to the right man."

It was several days before the Marquis of Worthington could manage to work a call on Lady Elizabeth into his busy schedule. When the time came, he found himself facing this duty with distinctly ambivalent feelings. On the one hand, being a man of his word, he fully intended to keep his promise to his father. But on the other, having a very good memory, he was finding the prospect of confronting his childhood nemesis rather disconcerting.

He chuckled at himself. "Remember, man, you've faced old Boney's soldiers. What can a mere woman do to you?" Unfortunately, he had several rather painful memories of what *this* woman had done — and that when she'd been only a child.

He descended from the barouche and surveyed the Farrington house. Well kept. All in order. At least she was doing a good job there.

He made his way to the front door and lifted the heavy brass F that served as a knocker. It was time to face the dragon in her lair.

The butler's bland face remained expressionless, but he ushered the marquis in with due solemnity. "Milady is in the study," the butler said. "If you'll just wait a moment."

Worthington nodded. Perhaps she would refuse to see him. Remembering how contrary she had been, that seemed a distinct possibility. He was trying to decide how he would feel about such an occurrence when the butler returned.

"This way, please, milord. Lady Elizabeth is at work."

So that's what she calls it, Worthington thought, pausing halfway through the study door. The room was a perfect shambles. Every flat surface held some oddity of nature. They hung from the ceiling, festooned the corners of cabinets, and were slung in the most haphazard fashion from every available projection. In one corner a life-sized wax effigy of a wild savage stared at him from fierce marble eyes. In another, what looked like a Medusa-figure glared out from under snaking hair. And in the center of the room, bent over a huge table and scarcely less terrifying, was the young woman he had come to see.

"The Marquis of Worthington," the butler intoned, and made his departure.

Her hair had turned darker, Worthington

noted, a rich auburn. She looked up. Blue-gray eyes shone out of a face of such angelic beauty that he could not believe what he was seeing. Mitchell had said beautiful, but he had expected a brittle, artificial beauty, buttressed and supported by fashion. This woman, wearing a simple day gown of pale green, would be lovely even in rags. "I — you — we —"

She laughed, a silvery tinkling sound that was music to his delighted ears. "You, speechless? I should never have believed it."

She made a sweeping motion. "Come, Tom-Tom, don't stand there gaping. Sit down and tell me why you're here."

Tom-Tom. How could he have forgotten that ridiculous nickname? Or how much he'd hated it? He reached out, thinking to remove the head of a mop that lay on the nearest chair. And the mop growled.

Startled, he pulled back.

"Fufu doesn't like strangers," Elizabeth explained. She whistled between her teeth and the mop jumped down and scurried to hide behind her skirts.

He lowered himself gingerly into the chair, and folded his legs carefully out of the way.

"So," she said, giving him a warm smile. "How is your shoulder? I hear you behaved

16

quite heroically in Spain. I envy you the chance to fight like that."

He tried to gather his wits. She might look like an angel, but she was still the same outspoken little hellion she'd always been. "I do not think you would care for fighting," he replied. "Most of us don't. It's rather messy work."

She nodded. "And you are quite recovered?"

"My physician assures me so." His hand went automatically to his shoulder, though at the moment it was not throbbing.

"But your wound still aches on occasion."

"Quite so."

The dog stuck its head out from behind her skirts and yapped at him. "Is that creature part of your exhibit?" he asked.

She laughed again. "Of course not. Have you changed so much that you no longer love dogs?"

"Of course not." He echoed her tone. "But my dogs are working animals. They earn their keep."

"So," she replied, "does Fufu."

She lapsed into silence then, gazing at him from those great blue-gray eyes with a directness that would have put most ladies to the blush. The silence stretched on and on, until at last, unable to bear her con-

17

tinued scrutiny, he blurted out, "I have come because I made my father a promise."

Her lovely mouth began to tighten and, wishing this well behind him, he hurried on. "I promised him I would look out for you."

"There is no need," she said briskly. "I can handle my own affairs."

"Yes, indeed. But a woman —"

Her eyebrows went up in an expression he remembered quite well, so well that involuntarily he drew back in the chair.

"This woman," she said with heavy emphasis, "is quite capable of managing her own affairs."

"But —"

She got to her feet and stood staring down at him. "You have no legal jurisdiction over me," she reminded him. "And I do not need your advice." Her expression softened. "Except perhaps on one matter."

He smiled. Thank goodness, she was going to be reasonable after all. "I shall give it gladly."

"Then come over here."

He got up and offered her his arm. But she had already turned and was picking her way through the chaos to a large table that stood against the wall.

He followed her and stood looking down at the strangest assortment of articles he had seen in some time. Skulls lay side-by-side with woven plaits of hair, odd-shaped bones, and dried herbs and flowers. And in the front, lined up like soldiers on parade, lay three shrunken heads, unmistakably human, their eyes staring at him in mute reproach.

He frowned. "Don't tell me you are still collecting such trash."

Her look threatened to annihilate him. "I know nothing of trash," she said with great dignity. "I am engaged in collecting scientific material for my museum."

He shook his head. "No, my dear Li—" Her hard look stopped him from using the nickname that had sprung automatically to his lips. "You are engaged in making a fool of yourself."

"What?"

When her hand closed around one of the heads and she swung round to face him, his reaction was automatic — and instantaneous. He retreated a step, tripped over something, and threw out his injured arm to steady himself. "Lizzie, stop! Don't throw it!"

"I do not throw precious scientific materials," she said with a glacial look.

What a fool he must appear! He dropped his arm, which now had commenced to throb again, and moved closer. "Quite wise," he said, trying a very small smile. "Some things are irreplaceable."

A smile pulled at the corners of her mouth. Funny, he'd forgotten how engaging her smile could be — even then, when he had thought her the bane of his youthful existence.

"I can't believe I really threw a shrunken head at you."

"Too bad I had no witnesses. You do remember pushing me into your father's fish pond?"

Her smile became full-blown, a lovely sight. "I wished to see if you could swim."

"After I had just told you I could not."

She shrugged. "I know. But I thought perhaps you were lying to me."

He tried to look affronted. "Why should I do that?"

"Because I had asked you to teach *me* to swim. As I remember it, learning to swim was the most important thing in my life at that moment."

"Well, I am sorry I had to disappoint you." He gave her the smile that in his heyday had earned him a reputation as the most eligible — and charming — connection in London. But the infuriating creature seemed not even to notice it.

"You *were* lying," she said. "I knew it then. And I'm sure of it now."

He laughed and conceded defeat. "Surely you can understand why. I could not take a fully clothed child into the fish pond."

Her smile was wicked. "Why, Tom-Tom, I was prepared to take off —"

"I know, I know." To his surprise, he felt a certain embarrassment. "But I could not allow that either."

"Then you should have told me the truth."

His smile became rueful. "As I recall it, the truth was not often what you wanted to hear."

She turned the full force of her smile on him again. "I am always reasonable," she said.

He wanted to laugh. Lizzie, reasonable? But he knew an opening when he saw one. "Then you will admit that this so-called museum of yours is a mistake."

"Mistake?" Her eyes blazed and her chin — quite a lovely chin, he noted in passing — came thrusting forward. "*I* do not make mistakes!"

"Oh yes, quite a reasonable attitude," he commented dryly. "Honestly, now, can't you see that people are laughing at you?"

She shrugged, drawing his eyes to a section of her anatomy that no gentleman would ever regard, at least not openly. He brought his gaze quickly to her face. "Why must you persist in this folly?"

"It is not folly," she said, her voice so even that he eyed her suspiciously. "It had long been Papa's dream to start such a museum. I have no children, no husband —"

He snorted. "A husband would never allow such a thing."

"Perhaps . . . perhaps not. In any case, I have no husband, and no one can stop me."

Her logic was just as confusing as always. But unfortunately, she was right in one particular: he could not do anything to stop her. He sighed. "What was it you wished my advice about?"

Her smile was pure sweetness. And should have served as a warning to him. "It's these heads. I am debating whether to display them together or singly. Tell me, what is your opinion?"

He stared at her, his ire rising. "You are asking my advice on shrunken heads?"

She bit her bottom lip. He remembered the gesture, designed to hold back laughter. "Yes, milord," she said. "I consider you an expert on the subject."

He didn't know whether to laugh or be affronted. A throb of pain from his afflicted shoulder decided him in favor of the latter. He had had enough of this inanity for one day. "I'm afraid you'll have to do without my advice," he said stiffly. "I have other matters to attend to."

Her face changed. The Lizzie he remembered disappeared before his very eyes and was replaced by a proper lady he didn't know at all. "Of course," she said politely. "I have taken up enough of your valuable time. It was kind of you to call, but, as you can see, I have no need of your assistance."

He nodded again. "Then I shall take my leave."

Elizabeth watched him make his way to the door. What a shame the war had changed him so. She remembered a boy full of fun and mischief. She smiled — a boy willing to be led into varied and exciting escapades. But, now that she came to think of it, *she* had done the leading.

Too bad about that wound. But how fortunate he had not been disfigured. He had quite an attractive face — even though his nose tended to the hawkish and his chin bespoke a stubborn temper. The rest of him was quite pleasant to look at, too — his clothes of the latest fashion, but not too ostentatious, his linen scrupulously clean. And that lean, dark look of his must have already set the London misses wild.

Yes, he had changed. She remembered fun and laughter, pranks and peccadillos. Now he was such a sobersides.

She sighed. The war with Napoleon had cost some men their limbs, others their lives. Tom-Tom had been lucky to come home whole and hearty. In body, if not in spirit.

She stooped and picked up the little dog. How coldly the man had made his farewell. "I suppose I must remember to address him as Worthington now," she told Fufu, scratching behind his ears. "It seems that Tom-Tom and Lizzie are only pleasant memories. Their friendship is no more."

Somewhat to her surprise, she discovered her eyes filling with tears. "Stupid dust," she muttered. "Now I can't see to work." She yanked at the bell pull. "Barton!"

"Yes, milady?"

"Tell Elias to get the carriage ready. Tomorrow we go to Madame Nuranova's camp."

Chapter Two

Later that afternoon Worthington looked up from the treatise on land reform that he was reading. "Caroline," he said to his sister. "Why don't you play for me?" She was fidgeting about the room like a green soldier before his first battle. "Come, come," he said. "There's no call to be nervous of the Viscount Vidon."

"I am not nervous," Caroline said, tossing her dark curls. "Not at all."

"Then why don't you sit down and do something? Play the piano. Sketch a picture." He looked pointedly at the volume he held. "Read a book."

Caroline threw up her hands. "Those are all such boring acts, so inconsequential."

He frowned. He'd had enough female logic for one day. "Most of life is inconsequential."

"I know. And I so long for some excitement." Her eyes sparkled as she spun to face him. "Oh, how I wish I could be in Spain."

He scowled. Had these women no sense? "War is a very painful experience," he said brusquely. "I can assure you, you would not like it."

She shrugged. "Perhaps not. But I still think men have all the fun."

He was tempted to tell her that there was precious little enjoyment in the various duties men had pressed upon them. Take that spitfire Lizzie. One could hardly call looking out for her *fun*. She was quite enjoyable to look *at,* though. Imagine that brat growing up into such a beautiful woman.

"Worthington!" Caroline cried. "I have already asked you twice."

"Asked me what?"

"How often the Viscount Vidon will be coming to call."

"As often as he likes."

"But he's *your* friend. Why must I be here?"

He stifled an exclamation of disgust. "Because it is *you* he's calling upon."

"But I don't wish —"

"It's too soon," he interrupted, "for you to know your own wishes. Vidon is a good man. The best."

"We fought side-by-side," she mimicked. "Can't you understand? I don't care about the viscount."

He tried to keep his patience, which, never in great reserve, had been sorely tried by the events of the day. "You have not taken the time to know him. When you do —"

"I shall still *not* want him for a husband." She gazed at him in distress. "Worthington, how can I make you understand? I want to *feel*, to feel something special when *he* walks into the room. To hear the earth sing and my blood sing with it."

For some unfathomable reason he had a vision of Lizzie's face. "What a load of drivel!" he exclaimed. "The meanderings of poets."

She glared at him indignantly. "Poets are the unacknowledged legislators of mankind. They show us the way."

"Where *are* you hearing such nonsense?" he demanded.

"It's truth, that's what it is. The new poet, Shelley, he says it. *He* is a legislator."

With difficulty, Worthington restrained his tongue. Had all of womankind gone suddenly mad? But no, there was the Little Dove. She knew a woman's place and how to fill it. His thoughts drifted to his homecoming visit with her. Soothing, pleasant thoughts.

"The Viscount Vidon," the butler announced.

Worthington looked to the door. "Vidon.

Come in." He surveyed his friend with a critical eye. Nothing amiss there. A good sturdy fellow, well turned out, but not foppish. What more did the girl want?

"Good afternoon," said Vidon, presenting Caroline with a large and — from the look of it — expensive bouquet. "Flowers for one more beautiful than any blossom."

A nice turn of phrase, Worthington thought, though he was sure he had heard it before; in fact, he'd probably used it himself.

But Caroline was definitely not impressed. "Thank you," she said, without so much as a smile.

Vidon looked uncomfortable, as well he might at such cavalier treatment. "Have I guessed wrong?" he inquired. "You do not *like* flowers?"

Caroline shrugged. "Oh, these are well enough. It's just that they're rather gaudy."

Worthington stifled an impulse to commit an act of mayhem on his ungrateful sister. "Caroline," he said warningly.

She had the grace to flush. "You're very kind, milord. It's just that, well, I prefer the simpler blossoms — like violets."

Vidon nodded. "I quite understand. That's very good thinking on your part."

"If you'll just excuse me," Caroline said, clutching the bouquet to her, "I'll go have these put in water."

"Not an auspicious beginning," observed Vidon, the moment the door closed behind her.

Worthington forced a smile. "She's a mere chit. She doesn't know her own mind."

Vidon shook his head. "It appears to me that she knows it quite well. And that she's taken a definite dislike to me."

"Nonsense, old —"

The butler appeared in the doorway. "Lady Linden and Miss Martine Linden."

Worthington frowned. Less than a week out of his country sickbed and only a few days in the city, and already he had the old gossip on his trail.

He sighed. "Show the ladies in. And tell my sister they are here." He turned to his friend. "Sorry, Vidon, I didn't expect —"

"I shall survive," said the viscount with a smile. "But only barely."

"Milord, how nice to see you up and about." Lady Linden's smile was as false as the curls piled so lavishly under her fashionable bonnet. And, since her ample figure was sheathed in a gown of meager proportions, she looked in dire danger of spilling out of it.

"Thank you," he replied, hoping they would avoid such a catastrophe. "I assure you, I, too, am pleased that I can be up and about."

The daughter, trailing behind her, was thin everywhere the mother was not. A stickish girl, her principal entertainment seemed to be taking a mental inventory of the contents of his study. Her eyes darted everywhere — from the Reynolds over the fireplace to the Sèvres porcelain on the mantel. He could almost see her adding up the figures in her head.

Though the daughter had been still in the schoolroom when he'd gone off to war, he had suffered the mother's visits too often to have forgotten them. And he suspected the daughter was just as greedy as the mother in gathering the misfortunes of others.

"Yes," Lady Linden cooed, settling herself in a lyre-backed chair that he could only hope would hold her. "Such a hero you are."

Fortunately, Caroline chose that moment to reenter the room and he was spared the embarrassment of responding to such effusions. "See," he told his sister, with rather more cheerfulness than the occasion warranted, "Lady Linden and her daughter have come to call."

He could see Caroline trying to muster some enthusiasm and in this case he could surely sympathize with her. "How kind of you," she murmured.

Lady Linden smiled. "I was just telling your dear brother how pleased we are to have him returned to us. All the young ladies have been dying to see him. Is that not so, Martine?"

The daughter jumped — disturbed, no doubt, in her calculations. "Of course, Mama. He is said to be the best connection in town."

Since he had not been upon the town for some four or five years and had, until this very afternoon, never laid eyes on Miss Linden, he found this piece of flattery rather fulsome. Still, he supposed, politeness might call for a certain exaggeration.

"So," he said. "And how have you ladies been amusing yourselves?"

"We have been out calling," said Martine eagerly. "And we have heard the most shocking things."

She did not look shocked, he observed. She looked quite invigorated. "Indeed," he replied, in what he meant to be a discouraging tone.

Evidently she did not notice his tone. "Oh yes," she hurried on. "Carol Lamb has been

31

chasing Lord Byron all around London. And her a married woman!"

"Lord Byron writes quite beautiful poetry," Caroline observed quietly.

Miss Linden dismissed such things with a shrug. "I do not read poetry." Her expression turned avid. "And then we heard about Lady Melbourne's newest — interest. And they say the Prince Regent —"

"Perhaps," said Worthington with a frown, "we should speak of other subjects. These are hardly fit matters for feminine tongues."

Across the room Vidon coughed and Worthington could almost hear his laughter. Well, let his friend think him stuffy. But with Caroline present . . .

"Well," said Lady Linden, "there's one thing we *can* talk about. Absolutely everyone in the city is."

"And what is that?" asked Caroline, obviously striving for politeness.

"Why, Lady Elizabeth's foolish museum."

Miss Linden's pinched features flushed with color. "They say that she means to have astonishing things in it. Shrunken heads and skeletons." She turned to him. "Milord, isn't that scandalous?"

"Quite," observed Worthington, though he was tempted to add that the practice of spreading gossip was even more reprehensible. At least Lizzie was forthright, honest. She did not go about spreading rumor and battening on others' misfortunes.

"It really is quite awkward," Lady Linden agreed, shifting her weight so that the delicate chair creaked in protest. "A lady doing such a strange thing. Why, it makes us all look poorly. Puts us all in ill repute."

Ill repute, indeed. As though running about London with a mouth full of damaging *on-dits* was the proper pastime of a lady.

Why, Lizzie was worth ten of this puffed-up dowager. And twenty of the stickish daughter with the crass soul of a merchant.

He was trying to think of some polite way to convey his displeasure with this sort of talk when Caroline said, "I think Elizabeth's behavior is quite admirable."

Four mouths fell open and four pairs of eyes turned to view Caroline in disbelief. Worthington closed his mouth with a snap. This conversation had gone far enough.

But before he could intervene Lady Linden said, "My dear Lady Caroline, whatever makes you say such a ridiculous thing?"

Caroline colored, but she held her ground. "The museum was her papa's dream. And it will advance the cause of science." She looked to her brother. "Worthington, you have always said that science is the hope of the future. Don't you still believe that?"

Worthington hesitated. He had said that very thing, but he had been thinking of discoveries like the new gas street lights and other such improvements, not the display of natural atrocities that Lizzie seemed to be contemplating.

"Well," demanded Lady Linden. "What *do* you believe?"

Several rather ripe curses rose to his lips, but he swallowed them and took the gentlemanly route. "I think that Lady Elizabeth's interest in science is quite admirable."

Lady Linden leaned forward precariously. "And you do not intend to stop her?"

"I?" Surprise made his eyebrows rise precipitously. "Good Lord, no!"

Lady Linden smiled, the smile of a cat discovered beside an empty canary cage. "I told you so, Martine. She will go to visit that nasty gypsy and come back with more things for her folly."

Worthington felt the Worthington temper beginning to rise. Why hadn't Lizzie told him she was going on a journey? The answer to that was easy: because, of course, he would have tried to deter her. A spasm in his injured shoulder made him grit his teeth. "Why," he asked, striving to keep his displeasure out of his voice, "should anyone think *I* would attempt to stop her?"

Lady Linden smiled coquettishly, an effort completely lost on him. "Why, milord, everyone knows you promised your father you would look out for her. And all of London has been waiting for you to recover from your wound and come to the city. So we could see the outcome of the contest between you." Her eyes sparkled. "I hear the odds at White's are three-to-one."

"Then the wagerers shall be disappointed," Worthington said, hanging onto his temper, though with some difficulty. "For I do not intend to interfere with Lady Elizabeth's —"

"The odds are three-to-one that Lady Elizabeth will be the winner," Lady Linden interrupted with a decided gleam of merriment in her eyes.

He felt his bad temper burgeoning into full-blown rage. "There will be *no* winner," he growled, grabbing at his throbbing shoulder, "because there will be no contest!"

A glimpse of Vidon's startled face recalled him to himself. He must be careful what he said. Every word would be repeated about the city, no doubt with extensive embellishments. He managed an excuse of a smile. "I am sorry, ladies, but I must ask you to leave now. As you know, I am but recently risen from my sickbed. And I find that too much excitement aggravates my wound."

"Of course, milord." The angular Miss Linden gazed at him with adoring eyes. And her mother's were equally approving. Now, why couldn't Lizzie look at him —

"We understand completely," said Lady Linden, in a tone he found decidedly offensive. She heaved herself to her feet. "Good day, milord. And good luck." She chuckled. "My money is on you."

Worthington occupied himself with the temper-containing habit of silently counting to ten, but he had actually reached ninety-nine before the door was safely closed behind his departing guests.

"Merciful heavens," exclaimed Vidon. "What a pair of harpies those two are!"

Caroline gave him a smile. "Elizabeth is a fine woman. It makes me so angry when they say these awful things about her."

"You have met her?" Worthington inquired, his gaze going to his sister in surprise. What had occurred here during his long absence?

"Of course. I first made her acquaintance at my come-out. Papa told me how you and she used to play together. And so I was eager to meet her."

Her face took on the stubborn expression he knew so well. "It's dreadful to have all these women talking about her. She was most kind to me. She — she helped me avoid a big mistake."

Worthington was instantly alert. "Mistake?" he repeated. "What mistake?" He was beginning to wish himself still fighting Napoleon. There, at least, one knew what to expect.

Caroline cast a look at Vidon. "I — I was enamored of a man. Papa disapproved of him." She gave Worthington a defiant look. "So I meant to run off."

"Great galloping cannonballs!" he shouted. "Why did no one tell me of these things?"

"Perhaps I should leave —" the viscount began.

"No, no. Stay." Worthington glared at Caroline. "Come, out with it now. What happened?"

Caroline looked miffed, but she said calmly enough, "Nothing happened. And that is precisely why you heard nothing about it." She stared at him. "When Papa wouldn't listen, I went to Elizabeth for help. She came up with a plan. She said it would show Papa that the man really loved me, that he was not a fortune hunter."

She sighed, but her gaze remained on his face. "Actually, it was a very good plan. Except that *I* was the one who learned the truth. When he heard that I had no dowry, the man fell suddenly out of love with me. So you see, Elizabeth saved me from a bad marriage."

Imagine Lizzie doing that. "But only because her advice was wrong," he pointed out.

Caroline leaped to her feet, her face twisted in disgust. "Really, Worthington, I begin to think your brain was injured as well as your shoulder! Elizabeth knew all along that the fellow was no good. But she also knew that I could not just be told that. I had to be shown."

Worthington digested this for a few moments. Unfortunately, the chit was right. "Then I'm sure you were appropriately grateful."

"Of course I was."

He tried for a reasonable tone. "So you need not go about London now, defending her."

Caroline shook her head. "I had thought

better of you," she cried. "Of course I shall defend her! She is my friend."

She turned to Vidon. "If you'll excuse me, milord. I find a dreadful headache coming on."

"Of course," said Vidon sympathetically. "You just run along and take a powder for it."

"You're most kind." Turning on her heel, she hurried out, almost careening into the steward, who was just coming through the door.

"Oh, do get out of my way!" she cried, hurrying on.

Mitchell turned and looked after her in bewilderment.

Worthington sighed. "There is no understanding women," he observed. "It is best not even to make the attempt."

Chapter Three

"I don't know why you persist in such things," Nanny whined from her corner of the carriage, fanning herself vigorously. "Gypsies is best left alone."

Elizabeth sighed and looked to the young woman who shared the squabs with her. "Sarah does not think so, Nanny. She is as excited as I."

Since Sarah Calvert was a poor relation, entirely dependent upon Elizabeth for her living, Nanny greeted this information with the sniff it deserved. Sarah, however, smiled. "Really, Elizabeth. Nanny knows that I am in agreement with her."

Elizabeth chuckled. "Then isn't it fortunate that I am the one in charge? Why, the two of you would stay safely at home and never see a bit of the world."

" 'Twould be wonderful," Nanny whispered, in such piteous tones that Elizabeth exchanged a smile with her companion.

" 'Twould be dreadfully dull," Elizabeth replied, in a Nannylike tone.

Nanny frowned. "I can't see why you

want to be dealing with gypsies." Her voice dropped to a whisper and her eyes widened. "They thieve babies, they do."

"Oh, Nanny, you *are* being silly. Besides, we have no babies to steal."

"They steal other things, too," Nanny said darkly. "You'll see."

Sarah sighed, her plain young face reflecting her concern. "Really, Elizabeth, you know the *ton* is all atwitter over your museum. And this trip will make them talk even more."

Elizabeth frowned. "What will it matter? They've been talking about me for years. And I've gotten along quite well. There is not a single member of the *ton* whose opinion means a thing to me."

For some strange reason, she had a mental picture of Worthington's face. But of course, she didn't care what *he* thought. This war with Napoleon had made him old before his time. And his attitudes about women were positively abhorrent. Telling her he meant to look out for her. As though she needed a keeper!

"Quit frowning so," Nanny admonished automatically. "You will give yourself wrinkles, you know."

Elizabeth forced herself to stop frowning. But her thoughts had taken a turn that made her uneasy. Worthington had been quite a stubborn boy. Once set in his ways, it had been almost impossible to budge him. And if he had promised his father —

"There it is," exclaimed Sarah. "I see the gypsy camp!"

Elizabeth leaned over to look. "How colorful the tents are."

Nanny gave another sniff and drew even further back into her corner. "I'm going to sit right here in this carriage," she declared, arms akimbo. "I ain't setting foot among such heathen."

Elizabeth smiled calmly. The years had taught her how to deal with the old nurse. "Very well, Nanny. But what a shame. Madame Nuranova may invite us to take tea with her. Wouldn't a nice cup of hot tea taste good about now?"

Nanny leaned forward a little. "Hot tea?" she repeated wistfully, licking her lips. "I am feeling a mite thirsty. Just a mite, you understand. My mouth gets dreadful dry from all this traveling."

Elizabeth saw Sarah biting her bottom lip and knew she was trying not to smile. "Well," Elizabeth said, "you do just as you think best."

By that time the carriage had come to a halt. Elias opened the door. "We're here," he said abruptly.

"Thank you, Elias." Elizabeth was used to the coachman's blunt ways. She knew they covered deep feelings of concern for her.

She also knew that he was just as offended by her choice of destination as Nanny. She sighed. Contrary to what some people might think, she didn't enjoy upsetting Elias. Or Nanny, either. But the museum meant a great deal to her; it was all she had. And she felt about it as she supposed a mother might feel about a beloved child.

Elias let down the steps, his weatherbeaten face reflecting dissatisfaction. "You'd best stick close to the carriage," he said softly. "I don't like the looks of this place."

Since Elias had more than once pulled her out of the suds, she usually paid attention to him. But this time she felt he was definitely wrong. The scene before her was lovely. Brightly draped tents lined one side of the meadow. Further down, men were shoving willow branches into the ground in half circles. The branches would, she knew, be covered with other branches and blankets — to make the shelters the gypsies called "benders."

In the middle of the meadow a small

campfire burned. Several men sitting near it discussed something about which, considering their waving arms and loud voices, they felt very deeply. Near one wagon a young woman with a baby on her hip stirred something steaming in a big iron kettle.

"You have come," said a deep, throaty voice. "We welcome you."

Madame Nuranova was a small woman of perhaps thirty, or forty. It was hard to say. To Elizabeth, she seemed to have always looked the same. Her coal-black hair hung far down her back, and eyes almost as dark peered out from a swarthy face.

"Thank you," Elizabeth replied. "We are pleased to be here."

The gypsy made a sweeping gesture with one dark hand and the gold bangles she wore at wrists, ears, and throat tinkled. "This, this is our camp for now. When we tire of it, we move on."

Elizabeth nodded. It seemed like a lovely idea: a life of freedom, no rules to restrict a person. But common sense promptly told her that every society, every group of people, had some rules. And for all she knew, the gypsy rules might be even more irksome than those of the *ton*. Though that hardly seemed likely.

"You have come far," Madame Nuranova

said graciously. "We go to my tent. You rest there."

"It is kind of you to receive us," Elizabeth said, as they started across the meadow, Nanny and Sarah trailing behind.

Madame Nuranova's eyes gleamed. "Your father, he was friend to us. Many times he gives us leave to camp on his land. Sometimes he protects us from those who want to harm us." She touched Elizabeth's arm lightly. "We are people of honor. We do not forget our friends."

By this time they had reached the tent, the most colorful of them all. A small table sat in a patch of shade. The gypsy queen motioned to the stools around it. "You sit," she said to Elizabeth and Sarah. She glanced at Nanny. "You want rocking chair?"

Nanny hesitated. It was plain she would love such a chair, but would she stoop to let a heathen provide it? She sighed and capitulated. "I — Yes, thank you. That carriage jolts most fearful."

Madame Nuranova chuckled. "Our bones, they grow old. I bring you good chair."

In a minute she was back, with a brightly painted, deeply cushioned chair. Nanny settled into it with a heartfelt sigh. "You're a kind creature," she said.

The gypsy winked at Elizabeth. "You are friend, too. All friends of Elizabeth's are friends of gypsies. This fair one, name of Sarah, she is very good friend."

Sarah looked up, surprised no doubt that the gypsy knew her name.

Madame Nuranova poured Nanny a cup of steaming tea from the fine china pot that stood on the table. Then she served the young women. And finally she filled a cup for herself and sat down. "Yes," she said to Sarah. "You are very good friend. For this I tell your future. No charge."

Sarah colored. "I'm afraid I know my future. I shall be a spinster."

Madame Nuranova reached across the table. "I look at your hand. I tell you what is to come."

"I —"

"Oh, Sarah," Elizabeth urged. "Do go ahead. Then I shall let her tell mine."

Sarah was plainly not enthusiastic. But she took off her glove and allowed the gypsy queen to peer into her palm. The gypsy's golden hoop earrings swung back and forth as she shook her head. "You are wrong. I see husband here. Children. Happiness."

Sarah's mouth had fallen open, and she stared down at her hand. "But it can't be. I've no dowry. Nothing. I —"

46

The gypsy frowned. "The hand does not lie. You will see."

Sarah sipped her tea thoughtfully. She looked, Elizabeth thought, almost as though she believed the fortune-teller. And that was good. Perhaps some man *would* appreciate Sarah's sterling qualities. She had always thought her friend would make an excellent wife.

Feeling adventuresome, Elizabeth leaned forward. "What about me, Madame Nuranova? Is there a husband in *my* future?"

Nanny's rocking chair began to creak, but Elizabeth did not turn to look. She stared into the gypsy's dark eyes.

"For this," said the gypsy. "I use the crystal ball." She reached under the table and brought it out. "In this, only *I* see," she said. "You be silent. You close eyes."

Obediently Elizabeth closed her eyes. Perhaps it was foolish, but she wanted to believe in the gypsy. It would be wonderful if Sarah could know happiness. And for herself, she wished . . .

"I see —"

"Yes, yes, what do you see?"

"I see man, dark man. Brave man. Angry man." Madame Nuranova stopped.

"Please," Elizabeth cried. "Oh please, go on."

47

The gypsy sighed. "I don't like to tell."

Elizabeth swallowed. "Please, what is it?"

"There is love. But there is trouble. Much fighting. Much anger."

"And?" Elizabeth asked, her heart threatening to choke her.

Madame Nuranova's voice grew thoughtful. "This man carries something. I cannot see what it is. He carries it to you." There was another pause. Then the gypsy laughed. "Yes, the end is good! I see happiness."

Elizabeth's eyes flew open. The breath she'd been holding came out in a great *whoosh*. "You mean I am to have a husband, too?"

The gypsy nodded emphatically. "Yes. Good husband. Much love."

Elizabeth turned. "Nanny, did you hear that?"

But Nanny, worn out from the long ride, had fallen asleep in her chair, the empty teacup clutched tightly in her fingers.

Some time later Elizabeth looked up from the box of natural curiosities Madame Nuranova had offered for her inspection. A gypsy man was approaching. "Men come," he told the queen. "Rich men. In rich carriage."

48

The gypsy queen drew herself up. "We have permission to be on this land. We do no wrong."

Still, Elizabeth could see that she was apprehensive. It must be difficult to be treated like a pariah — and just because one's background was different. Papa had always said it took all kinds to make a world. And he had meant it, treating everyone, rich or poor, English or foreign, with the same polite respect. But Papa had been an unusual man.

A carriage stopped by the side of the meadow. As the first man stepped down, Elizabeth experienced the strangest feeling of familiarity. Then she realized why. Worthington! What on earth was *he* doing here?

His face looked thunderous. She knew the signs of a storm blowing up. Getting to her feet, she faced him. "Good day, milord. What are you doing here?"

Worthington was not in the best of moods. The jiggling of the carriage had irritated his shoulder, which had now begun to throb like a toothache. The heat had made him feel weak and unsettled. And he was acutely aware of the stupidity of chasing about the countryside after a creature over whom he had no control at all. "I have come because of you," he said, with difficulty resisting the urge to give her a good shaking.

He had done so more than once when they were children and, as he remembered, he had not fared particularly well then, either. Of course, shaking her now, grabbing her and holding her close — He stopped that line of thought abruptly. This wasn't the little Lizzie of his childhood. This was a grown woman.

She was standing there, smiling at him gravely, entirely at ease, as cool and composed in her peach-colored gown as if she'd stood in her own drawing room. While he, hot and probably fevered, was feeling like some kind of awkward, ill-bred pup. "I came," he said sternly, "to protect your repu—"

Her eyebrows started to go up and her foot to tap, and he stopped and changed direction. "The *ton* is talking," he began again. "Everyone is whispering about your museum."

She shrugged. "*Everyone* should mind his own business. As I do." She turned away, toward the table spread with assorted strange objects, then stopped and turned back. "Excuse me, Sarah. Worthington, this is my friend, Sarah Calvert. Sarah, the Marquis of Worthington."

50

"Miss Calvert," he said, bowing a little. At least the companion looked the sensible sort. "And this is my friend, the Viscount Vidon."

Vidon smiled at the ladies. "You must forgive my friend," he said. "His shoulder still pains him. Ordinarily he is as tame as a pussycat."

Trust Vidon to inject a little humor. The plain young woman named Sarah smiled. "I am sure the war was very difficult," she said sweetly.

Vidon took her arm and led her a short distance away. "Let me tell you . . ." he began.

Worthington looked again to Lizzie. "This is no simple matter we are faced with," he said, trying for a calm tone and failing miserably. "Lady Linden came to call."

Lizzie's nose wrinkled in distaste. "That creature has the morals of an alley cat."

He stifled a smile. "Perhaps so. She was equally quick to comment on yours."

She bridled. "Don't be ridiculous. My morals are above reproach."

"Lady Linden doesn't think so. She says you put your whole sex in ill repute."

"What a lot of foolishness."

Her eyes sparkled in the sunlight and he

51

liked the way her chin — Good Lord, he shouldn't be thinking about her chin, not when she was continually getting them into the suds like she did. "We have also made the betting book at White's," he went on.

She gave him a strange look. "We have? How?"

"They're laying odds on whether or not I can stop you from —" He saw his mistake, but too late.

"Let them! I don't care." She glared at him defiantly. "And I shall not be stopped."

"I do not intend to try," he returned. "But this traveling about the countryside alone —"

"I am not alone. I have Sarah and Nanny. And Elias."

"Two women and an old man."

"Elias will not thank you for that."

"Nevertheless, it's true. There are still highwaymen about, you know. And returned soldiers who cannot find work."

She drew herself up and looked him in the eye. "I have been perfectly safe for four-and-twenty years. All without any assistance from you, I might add. And I shall continue to be safe in the same fashion."

He saw that he had bungled the whole thing. This fever had addled his wits. Otherwise he would have known Lizzie couldn't be reasoned with. "I told you about my promise —"

"You had no right to make it."

"He was dying! What if on his deathbed your Papa had asked —"

"He did," she cried triumphantly. "He asked me to build his museum!"

Chapter Four

Elizabeth almost laughed aloud. Never had she seen a more astonished expression appear on a man's face.

"He didn't!" he cried.

"Oh, but he did." Poor Tom-Tom. He looked really pale. Suddenly, her mirth vanished. "Worthington, are you ill? Would you like to sit down?"

"I am quite well, thank you."

He spoke so stiffly that she felt like pinching him. What she wouldn't give to have her old childhood friend back — even for a few minutes. "I *do* wish you would not be such a boor about this. Is there not some way we can come to an agreement?"

He rubbed his shoulder. "I do not see how. I cannot go back on my word."

"Nor I on mine," she returned.

He frowned. "But we cannot go on this way, the laughingstock of all London."

She was used to being talked about. But she could see that he found it troublesome. "Then what shall we do?"

He shook his head. "I don't know. Let's

ask Vidon. In Spain, he worked with the diplomats. Where is the fellow, anyhow?"

"He's over there somewhere, talking to Sarah." Could Vidon be the man the gypsy had seen in Sarah's future? She looked so happy, so glowing. And he had appeared right after the prophecy. Elizabeth sighed. She was being silly, of course. Madame Nuranova could not really foretell the future. And yet —

"Vidon," Worthington called. "Come here, will you?"

While Sarah watched, the viscount listened to their problem. Then he smiled. "The solution is quite simple."

"It is?" Worthington frowned.

"Of course. You will *both* do as you promised."

"But —"

"Worthington, will you feel that you have fulfilled your promise to your father if you do look out for the lady?"

"Of course, but —"

"And you, Lady Elizabeth, will you be satisfied if you can open your museum with no interference from the marquis?"

"Of course. But he cannot stop me anyhow." What was the man getting at?

The viscount nodded. "Here, then, is what you must do. Lady Elizabeth will continue with her work of collecting —"

"I cannot look out for her if she is skipping around the countryside," Worthington said in exasperation.

Vidon gave Worthington a hard look. "Lady Elizabeth will notify you whenever she means to travel. So that you may go along and protect her."

It was plain to Elizabeth that Worthington didn't care much for this arrangement. In truth, neither did she. But it *was* a way out. And perhaps he was not always in such a foul mood. "And you will not try to stop me?" she asked him.

"He will not," declared the viscount. "I shall guarantee it. For I shall be with him."

A quick glance at Sarah's glowing face convinced Elizabeth that the viscount was not without ulterior motives in this. But she would not mind that gentleman's company, especially if it made Worthington more amenable.

She turned to him. "And will you help me?" she asked.

Worthington frowned. "I — I suppose so," he said finally. "But I must have your word not to leave the city without giving me ample notice. I do not care for these hurry-up trips."

Elizabeth sighed, wishing again for the

old Tom-Tom, the fun one. This one was so sober, so serious. "I agree," she said. "You have my word."

"Very good," said the viscount, leading Sarah away.

Worthington stood like a man in a daze. "If you have a moment," she said, hardly knowing why she did so, except perhaps because he looked so lost, "I should like your opinion on some things."

He smiled then, and suddenly she was six years old again, gazing up at a boy she adored. It was a most startling feeling, but it was almost instantly gone and she had no time to think of it then.

"Of course," he replied. "I only hope these things do not include shrunken heads."

Some time later, Worthington watched Madame Nuranova put Lizzie's purchases carefully into a box and accept her gold. Far too much gold, to his mind.

He sighed. Vidon's suggestion had condemned him to following Lizzie wherever she went. And even worse, he had given his word not to try and stop her museum. Still, he could not have done that in any case. And there was his promise to his father. It was just that the Little Dove was waiting, and —

The gypsy reached across the table. "Take off glove," she said. "I tell future."

He shook his head. Such flummery was better left to — Then he saw Lizzie's face, wearing that sly grin he remembered so well. And even before she opened her mouth, he knew trouble was brewing.

"Afraid?" she asked.

"Of course not." His words came out a little louder than he intended. Why did she have such a peculiar effect on him?

"Then give Madame Nuranova your hand."

A hundred excuses raced through his mind, but each was less believable than its predecessor. And he knew she would find them laughable.

"She's already read Sarah's future," Lizzie said, with that smile that had always meant mischief. "And mine."

He raised an eyebrow. "Indeed. How exciting."

The dryness of his tone was not lost on her. He noted the spark in her eyes, but she merely smiled. "Yes, it was. We are both to have husbands, you see."

"Both . . ." He stopped himself. Sarah Calvert was plain, a commoner, and dowerless, to boot. She was not likely to be in great demand. But Lizzie —

"Come," she urged, her eyes dancing with mischief. "I wish to hear if you are to be married."

The prospect was appalling. "I? Married? I should think not."

Nevertheless, with her gaze upon him, he could do no less than strip off his glove and give the gypsy his hand. Her touch was light, strangely soothing.

"A good hand," she said, turning it this way and that. "Strong. You are brave man."

A little sound escaped Lizzie, but when he looked up, she was leaning forward, staring at the gypsy.

"I see danger," the gypsy went on. "Fighting. War. You are hurt." She nodded. "This is all past. Now I look at love line. In your life many women, but one deep love. And marriage. Yes, I see marriage."

He tried to pull his hand away, but her grip was firm. "You are wrong," he said stubbornly. "I do not intend to become leg-shackled."

The gypsy raised her head, her jet-black eyes peering into his. "You will see."

A frisson of belief ran up his spine and he laughed to cover his discomfort. "If I decide to marry, I shall certainly invite you to my wedding."

The gypsy did not laugh. She looked him

full in the face and said, "You shall marry. I shall come."

She left the table, then, and Lizzie looked at the sky. "It is getting late. We must start for home. I hate to tear Sarah away, but —"

Startled, he asked, "Tear her away from what?"

"Why, from the viscount. Surely you noticed how well they are getting on."

His shoulder now beat with a steady thud, his cravat, wilted as it was, threatened to choke him, and a dull ache was commencing at his temples. The day was rapidly disintegrating, going from bad to worse.

"You are mistaken," he said firmly. "The Viscount Vidon is paying court to my sister."

Lizzie's dismay was evident. "He can't! He is all wrong for her."

With difficulty, he hung on to his fraying temper. "You have only just met Vidon, and —"

"True. But I have known Caroline for some years. And I tell you seriously, Vidon is not the man for her."

He could no longer contain himself. "My sister is *my* concern," he shouted, causing heads to turn. "And I will thank you to leave her welfare to me."

"I should be glad to," she replied, her low

tone making him look — and feel — even more boorish, "when you are capable of understanding her."

"I do —" He decided to try another tack. "You must know that I wish my sister to marry well. I know Vidon. I trust him."

"Fine. Does Caroline love him?"

The question startled him. "Why on earth should that matter?"

She stared at him as though he had suddenly grown horns. "Why should it matter? Why, for a woman, love is everything."

He shrugged. "There's no need to make this into a tragedy. Vidon is a good chap. He has a title. He has —"

She raised an eyebrow. "A title? Are you telling me that having a title makes a man a fit husband?"

That was not precisely what he had in mind. Trust Lizzie to twist his words into something else! "No, I —"

"Well, let me tell *you*. For a woman in love, a title means nothing."

He stared at her. She couldn't mean —

"You — you would not marry a commoner?"

She glared at him. "For your information, milord, if I loved a man, I should marry him, even if — if he were a coachman!"

And off she stomped to her carriage,

calling to the others as she went.

It was almost a week later that Elizabeth decided to call upon Caroline. She did not intend to let a disagreement with Worthington interfere with her friendship for his sister. And besides, she had given her word to let him know about future trips. Perhaps, since the heat had abated, he would not be quite so irritable.

"Elizabeth! I am so glad to see you." Caroline looked up from her stitching and flashed a smile of welcome. "I was afraid . . ."

Elizabeth returned the smile and took a chair. "You didn't think I would let your brother keep me away?"

Caroline looked sheepish, as though she had thought exactly that. "Well, I just didn't know."

"It's true, your brother and I had a slight disagreement." Elizabeth frowned. "Actually, we disagree over many things. But this time —"

"He will not try to stop you?" Caroline cried in alarm. "From opening your museum?"

"No, dear. Not since I told him I promised Papa on his deathbed."

Caroline looked thoughtful. "Yes, he

would respect that. But I didn't know —"

"This time our argument was about love," Elizabeth continued. "Or, more precisely, about whether or not love is necessary for a good marriage."

Caroline sighed and looked up from her needlepoint. "He is the most obstinate man. Naturally, he said love isn't necessary."

Elizabeth nodded. "You're quite right. He said exactly that." She chuckled. "I'm afraid I rather offended him then."

Caroline smiled. "That is not difficult to do these days. The war has changed him so much."

"Yes, it has. But then, what I said was, I suppose, a trifle shocking."

Caroline raised an eyebrow. "It was? Whatever did you say?"

"I told him that if I loved a man, I should marry him even if he were a commoner — in fact, even if he were a coachman."

Caroline giggled. "No wonder he has been stomping around, muttering imprecations. Would you really do that? Marry a commoner, I mean?"

Elizabeth hesitated, but only for a moment. "Yes," she said. "If he was a good man and I loved him."

A peculiar expression crossed Caroline's face. "Yes," she said. "So should I. But can you imagine Worthington's reaction to such a thing?"

Elizabeth could, but she preferred not to. "He told me that Viscount Vidon has been coming to call. How do you feel about him?"

Caroline shrugged. "He is a good enough man, I suppose. But I do not want him for a husband. He doesn't make my heart sing."

Elizabeth nodded. She knew what Caroline wanted in marriage. "You are quite sure?"

"Oh yes!" Caroline eyed her curiously. "Why do you ask?" She paused, her eyes widening. "Oh, Elizabeth, are you —"

"No, no. The viscount doesn't make my heart sing, either. But Sarah is much taken with him. And apparently, he with her." She leaned forward, unable to keep the news to herself for another moment. "Madame Nuranova read our fortunes the other day. And guess what? She promised us both husbands."

Caroline's eyebrows went up. "Do you — believe her?"

Elizabeth sighed deeply. "I want to. I want to very much."

"Are you —" Caroline hesitated. "Have you —"

Elizabeth shook her head. "Not I. But

that very day, Worthington and the viscount showed up at the gypsy encampment. And the viscount went directly to Sarah. It was almost as though . . ."

Caroline's eyes widened. "And Worthington, was he upset?"

Elizabeth nodded. "Actually, in a way, it was that which precipitated our quarrel. He did not appreciate my telling him that Vidon was all wrong for you." She eyed her friend. "I do believe that, you know."

"Yes, I know. Oh, I hope he will develop a *tendre* for Sarah. She is such a good person."

Elizabeth chuckled. "And, of course, that would prevent him from courting you."

Caroline smiled, a little sadly, Elizabeth thought. "Listen, Elizabeth, I must talk —"

"Talk about what?" inquired Worthington from the doorway. Then he saw Elizabeth, and a strange expression crossed his face.

Caroline colored slightly. "About a gown I saw at Madame Dusard's. It had the most intriguing ruching."

"Well," said Worthington, "you will have to discuss the frivolities of fashion without me." He turned as though to leave.

"Wait," Elizabeth cried. "Please . . . I wish to speak to you."

"To me?" He turned back, looking a little startled.

"Of course." Caroline's talk of gowns and ruching had not fooled anyone but her brother. But whatever his sister wished to talk about would have to wait. Elizabeth intended to fulfill the terms of their agreement. And besides, it did not seem right for such old friends to be at outs.

Worthington came into the room and took a chair, stretching his long legs, in their fawn inexpressibles, out in front of him. They were very good-looking legs, she noted with a little surprise. And his bottle-green coat fit exceedingly well.

He offered her a tentative smile. "I had thought that perhaps — after the other day — you were never going to speak to me again."

How foolish could the man be? They had used to argue all the time. "Of course I shall speak to you. But I'm afraid that when I'm thwarted I sometimes have a little bad temper."

"A little," he replied dryly. "But then, I've been known to have a temper of my own."

Evidently, he considered that an apology. Under the circumstances, she decided to accept it as such. "I have come," she said, "in accordance with the terms of our agreement. To tell you I am making plans for my next trip."

From the startled look on Caroline's face, it appeared her brother had told her nothing of what had transpired at the gypsy encampment.

"You are going on another journey?" Worthington said.

Why must he look so annoyed? "Yes," Elizabeth went on, "there's a learned pig in a village north of here. I should like to see if it can really do the tricks credited to it."

"And if it can?"

"Then I wish to engage it for some performances at the museum." She wished he would not stare at her with such disdain.

"Why should you wish to put this so-called 'learned porker' in a scientific museum?"

Why must he be so obtuse? "The answer is simple enough. The pig will draw a crowd. They will watch him for a while, then go on to view the other exhibits."

He sighed like a man much put-upon. "And when do you propose to make this trip?"

"I thought perhaps Monday night. I came to tell you because I promised I would. But truly, Worthington, I know you are a busy man. There's no need for you to go along.

We shall manage quite well."

"Monday next is fine," he said. "I shall be at your door with my carriage at nine in the morning."

True to his word, Worthington and his carriage arrived on Monday morning. The Viscount Vidon, grinning broadly, helped the ladies in.

It was immediately apparent to Elizabeth that Worthington was out of sorts, perhaps because the viscount had already begun to converse with Sarah as though she were the only person present. Or perhaps because some other diversion of his had been delayed.

Elizabeth was pondering how best to address him, when, in not the politest of tones, he asked, "So, what is this porker supposed to do?"

"According to the handbill, he can spell, read, cast accounts —"

Worthington straightened and cast her a peculiar look. "What a Banbury tale! It's obviously some sort of trick."

She resisted the unladylike urge to make a face at him. Why did he always manage to bring out the worst in her? "Oh, but that is not all," she continued. "He can play cards, tell anyone what time it is — and that by their own watch — and tell the age of anyone in the company."

With each claim she uttered, his face grew more sour. Finally he looked so peculiar that she felt her laughter rising. She swallowed it hastily. Tom-Tom hated to be laughed at. "Perhaps we should wait until we see him," she said, and turned to Sarah.

They arrived at the village shortly before noon. And Worthington was glad of it. It was infuriating to see Vidon making a fool of himself over Sarah Calvert. Of course, she was a dowerless commoner, fair game, some peers might say, though he had never considered that the gentlemanly route. Nor had he thought Vidon the kind of man to lead such a woman on. And in front of Lizzie —

Now, what on earth had that to do with anything? He climbed out, surveyed the village, and frowned. Why couldn't Lizzie want something close at hand? Or, better yet, why couldn't she just forget this whole crazy museum idea?

All of London would be talking about them by now. With people like Lady Linden prowling about, no man's affairs were private.

He turned, but Vidon had already helped

the ladies down. Then, of course, the viscount offered Sarah his arm. Worthington sighed. He had either to offer Lizzie his arm or be thought extremely rude.

He struggled to bring forth a smile and did the gentlemanly thing. "Now, where is our learned friend?"

The pig, it turned out, was performing at the local inn. The inn yard was crowded, and *oohs* and *aahs* were issuing from the assembled villagers. Worthington cleared a path to the performance.

The pig was huge. And, thank goodness, clean. But to put such a creature in a museum —

"Now," said the pig's master, a country bumpkin if Worthington ever saw one, "Toby, you just spell out your name."

To Worthington's surprise, the pig selected a card from the rows before him and laid it at his master's feet. Three more and his name was complete.

"Toby!" cried the showman. "Toby, the smartest pig in all of England."

Lizzie leaned a little closer, pushed, no doubt, by the crowd. Worthington felt the warmth of her body against his side. How could her body be so beautiful, so soft, so feminine, and her mind so contrary? She was far more lovely than the Little Dove. If

Lizzie had been any other woman — with looks like hers — he would already have declared his admiration.

But she wasn't any other woman. She was Lizzie, the demon who'd made his childhood a chaos. He never knew what she would do next . . . or trick *him* into doing.

He considered this while the learned pig ran through his repertoire of tricks. And then the showman said, "That's all for now, folks. Toby's got to rest. Next show's at three o'clock."

The crowd drifted away and Elizabeth approached the showman. "Mr. Ware," she said, flashing a smile that would melt the hardest heart — unless, of course, its possessor knew her as Worthington did — "I have come to offer you an engagement in London. At the Farrington Museum."

Mr. Ware scratched his tousled head. "Ain't heard of that place."

"It's to open soon. Very soon. And you will be our star attraction."

Mr. Ware hesitated. "Toby, he's the country kind. Don't know as how he'd be happy in the city. Awful noisy and all." He grinned. "And no other pigs."

Lizzie smiled again. How could she smile like that at this country bumpkin whose pig looked cleaner than he did?

"I assure you, Mr. Ware, Toby will have excellent accommodations. There's a room in the back of the museum."

"He don't like being alone. Being he's the sociable kind."

Lizzie actually nodded. "Then you may stay with him. If you like, we need arrange only for one week's performances. But I'm confident you'll want to stay longer."

"Perhaps. But you ain't mentioned the fee."

"Why, that is up to you. Set a sum — so much for the week. And I shall pay it."

The showman's eyes grew crafty. And then he mentioned a sum that made Worthington's hackles rise. Surely she would not —

"That'll be fine," she said cheerfully. "My coachman will give you the direction. We'll expect to see you there, say, the first week in September."

"Right enough, milady. We'll be there." And off went Mr. Ware, the pig ambling at his heels.

"Have you lost your mind?" Worthington demanded.

She gave him that too-sweet smile. "I don't believe so, milord."

"But such an amount —"

"Assures me that the man will be there

when I need him."

"But —"

Her chin thrust out and her eyes took on that hard look he knew so well. "I do not wish to discuss the matter further." She slid her arm through his again. "Come, let us find Sarah and the viscount. I could use a cup of tea."

They had had their tea and were nearly back to London when Vidon said, "It's still early in the day. Why don't we go to Leadenhall Street, to the East India Company Museum?"

Elizabeth looked to Worthington. "His lordship is but newly out of his sickbed," she said. "He should not overexert himself."

"I have been fighting a war," he replied, in a surprisingly gentle voice. "I believe I can handle a walk through a museum."

"I only meant —"

His hand covered hers for the briefest instant. "I know what you meant," he said softly.

A blush spread to her cheeks. She could feel the heat of it. "There, there *is* something I'd like you to see," she murmured. "I wish I could have gotten it for my museum."

The corner of his mouth twitched. "Not —"

"No," she answered, now fully recovered. "Not another shrunken head."

When they arrived, the East Indian House Museum was not open to the public. But the curator said, "Lady Elizabeth, do come in. You and your friends take all the time you want."

She had to give Worthington credit. He seemed determined to look at everything. They wound their way through several long passages and up a narrow stairway, pausing in ill-lit rooms to consider the native weapons and farm implements of India, Burmese musical instruments, and fat little Buddha statues.

"A very interesting concept of the Almighty," Worthington remarked. "Is that what you wanted me to see?"

"No. It's further along. Here."

They turned a corner and Sarah gave a gasp of fright. Elizabeth had to concede that the life-sized figure of the tiger devouring a man was a trifle startling.

"Well," observed Worthington. "That is something worth seeing."

"It's called 'Tippoo Tiger,'" Elizabeth explained.

He eyed the mechanical contraption. "The fallen man appears to be English, from the look of that scarlet coat."

"Yes. Turn the crank. In the tiger's side."

He gave her a quizzical look.

"Please."

He shrugged and did as she asked. The tiger let out a deep-throated roar and the man figure gave an ear-splitting shriek. Then the tiger's head began to move and the man figure to writhe in agony.

"Quite a spectacle," Worthington commented dryly.

Elizabeth was not sure whether he referred to the tiger or to Sarah, hastily disengaging herself from the shelter of the viscount's waistcoat, to which the tiger's roar had sent her scurrying. "An Oriental potentate had it created," Elizabeth explained. "I suppose he wished all Englishmen to suffer a similar fate."

Worthington returned to her side and offered her his arm again. "At least he was honest in his opinion. No guile there."

"No. No guile." Was there some undercurrent to his words, something she was not catching? But she had not deceived him about anything, except perhaps — "Do you see why I wish I had it for my exhibits?"

"Oh, yes. It's very scientific."

That smile was there again, the one that reminded her of the way he had once been. "Come now, Tom-Tom —"

Vidon's head snapped around. "Tom-Tom?"

Worthington's face darkened. "A childhood nickname," he said, "one I'll thank you to keep private."

Vidon put on a placating expression. "Of course, of course."

Elizabeth hoped Vidon would not laugh. She should not have let herself make such a foolish mistake. But for a moment there, it had seemed like old times. "The marquis and I — we knew each other as children. In the summers —"

Worthington smiled. "In the summers, Lizzie led me into uncountable acts of mischief." To her surprise, she felt a little surge of warmth at his use of the old nickname. "She was very good at it, too."

"We were children," she began again.

The viscount nodded sagely. "We quite understand. Not a whisper of this shall pass our lips."

She knew Sarah would not divulge anything, but she was not so certain of Vidon. "Thank you," she said. "The *ton* has already talked about us far too much."

Worthington nodded. "Indeed, they have. But I suppose we had better get accustomed to it. Unless I miss my guess, we will both have visitors tomorrow."

"I shall not be at home," Elizabeth said. "I have a great deal to do before my museum opens."

Worthington nodded. "I'm sure you do. But don't forget Caroline. She'll be wanting to see you."

Chapter Five

Several days passed before Elizabeth could arrange time to call on Worthington's sister. As the carriage approached the house, Elizabeth found herself fidgeting on the seat. She was being ridiculous, she knew. There was no need to be fearful of Worthington. Really, she was not fearful; she was, well, she was a little anxious. After all, he could be a big help. Or he could be a thorn in her side. And lately, she just didn't know how to behave around him.

Until that day he had appeared in her study, she had thought of him only occasionally — pleasant thoughts of the childish adventures they'd shared. But now, he seemed to be in her mind constantly. She found herself wondering what *he* would do about this or that, what *he* would think of this or that. She sighed. If only she could bring back that wonderful boy she missed. True, they had fought like the proverbial cats and dogs. But somehow she had always known he was her friend.

Now he had become this man who

seemed sometimes friend and sometimes not. She supposed she could accept that. *If she could just forget their old friendship.* But she could not; old feelings kept interfering. And for the first time in her life, she was seriously thinking of — It must be the gypsy's prophesy that had put that foolishness in her head. He said he did not intend to marry. And he had always been a man of his word.

Enough of this kind of thinking. She had come to call upon Caroline, to discover — if possible — what her friend had been prevented from telling her last week. It had appeared rather serious then, and it had been preying on her mind since.

When Elizabeth entered the library, Caroline looked up from her sketchbook. "Hello. Do come in. Sit here by me."

Caroline was alone, Elizabeth saw, with mingled disappointment and relief. "What are you —"

Caroline closed the sketchbook abruptly. "Nothing. Nothing at all. Take off your bonnet."

Elizabeth complied. "Thank goodness the heat has abated for a while. How is your brother doing?"

Caroline looked a trifle amused. "He seems well enough. Though I cannot believe that he has agreed to help you with the museum."

"Does he say much about it?"

Caroline shook her head. "Not really. But he is so restless. Except —" Caroline colored. "Except, I suspect, when he has visited *her*."

Elizabeth's heart suddenly decided to hammer in a most irregular fashion. "Visited who?"

"Oh, Elizabeth, I should not have mentioned it. I thought you knew." Now Caroline looked embarrassed. "I know we women are not supposed to know about such things. It's the Little Dove. I heard he has set her up again. You know she was his . . . Well, you know how men are."

"Yes, I do know." Elizabeth pulled in a deep breath. Strange, how her heart had behaved like that. Of course Tom-Tom had a lightskirt. Every lord had one. Or just about.

Now, if he meant to get married — That must have been what set her heart to pounding so, the thought that he might get married and she would lose her friend altogether.

But she was here for a different purpose than to consider Worthington's future. She gave Caroline a searching look. "The other

80

day you were going to tell me something. Something important, I think."

Caroline turned so pale she looked almost ill.

"My dear, what is it?"

"You — you helped me before," Caroline whispered, her gaze on the door. "But — but this time, this time, I — I just don't know."

Elizabeth took her friend's hand. "I cannot help you if you don't tell me about it. Is it a man again?"

Caroline nodded. "Yes. And I love him so much." She blinked and her eyes widened in alarm. Then her whole expression swiftly changed. "Thank you, Elizabeth, the dizzy spell has passed."

"Dizzy spell?" Worthington repeated from the doorway.

Elizabeth turned, keeping her face calm and trying to think of some excuse. "It's probably an aftereffect of the heat."

Worthington frowned. "Shall we send for Dr. Higham?"

"No, no. I shall be all right." Caroline pressed a hand to her forehead. "It's passing."

"Very well, if you're sure." Worthington crossed the room. "It's good to see you," he said to Elizabeth. "How is your work going?"

His good humor so surprised her that she had to pull herself together to reply. "The work goes slowly, but it does progress."

"Fine." He settled into his chair. "I'm glad you've come to see Caroline. She has been looking rather pallid lately."

"Probably from the heat," Elizabeth offered. He had seemed willing to believe that before. "London summers can be quite debilitating."

He nodded. "Indeed, they can."

"It is not the heat," protested Caroline, with a forced little laugh, "it's the callers."

Elizabeth frowned. "I'm afraid I do not understand."

"People keep coming to call. And they ask me questions, endless questions."

"Questions?"

Worthington actually chuckled. "Questions about us," he said. "It seems we are the talk of the town."

She couldn't help it. She stared at him. "And you no longer mind this?"

He shrugged. "Why should I let such things disturb me?"

Across the room, out of his line of vision, Caroline was making flying motions with her arms and nodding wisely. The Little Dove. So, Elizabeth thought, this was how a man behaved when he had lately left his inamorata. No wonder such women got jewels and gold for their services.

"Have I something amiss about my person?" he inquired.

"No, no." Obviously her scrutiny of him had lasted too long. "I just thought — you are looking quite well today."

He smiled again. "And I am feeling well. Are you —"

"Lady Linden and Miss Martine Linden," the butler announced.

"Oh no!" Caroline put her hand to her mouth in dismay. Worthington's smile began to fade.

Elizabeth sighed. "I have not been at home to them all week."

He gave her a rueful look. "I'm afraid that dodge won't work here. No doubt they recognized your carriage. We shall all have to be at home today." He turned, ready to smile at their visitors. Composing her face, Elizabeth followed his lead.

Lady Linden had not decreased in size, Elizabeth noted as she came in. Nor had her sense of fashion improved. A mauve-and-yellow-striped gown was hardly the thing for a woman of such amplitude, and to make matters even worse, the stripes curved around her figure. She looked remarkably like one of Hogarth's caricatures.

"Why, Lady Elizabeth! We didn't expect to find you here," the older Linden said, with that patently false smile.

"Nor I you," remarked Elizabeth, with equally false politeness.

"We just stopped by to see dear Lady Caroline," trilled the younger.

"That's kind of you, I'm sure." Elizabeth debated. Should she plead another engagement and leave? If she left, they could hardly follow her. But they would know — or at least strongly suspect — that she wished to avoid them. Perhaps it was better to stay. To put a good face on it, as Papa would say. And besides, she had not yet discovered what she'd come to find out.

From his vantage point, Worthington surveyed the visitors. His hours with the Little Dove had imparted to life a rather rosy glow. He had actually been enjoying his conversation with Lizzie, feeling relaxed and contented. She was not half bad company when she wasn't going on about that museum.

But now these two had come to disturb his pleasant little world. Still, it would be interesting to see Lizzie in action. He had no doubt she was a match for these prosing talebearers.

He suppressed a sigh as Lady Linden descended onto his settee. At least that piece of furniture should hold her. If he was lucky.

"Don't you think so, milord?" The question was evidently addressed to him. Miss Linden was eyeing him with that look of doglike devotion which in a dog was admirable but in a young female definitely was not.

"I'm afraid," he confessed, "that I have been wool-gathering. I have been absent from my affairs for so long, you see, and there is so much to attend to." He gave them his most winning smile, rather wasted on such a pair, he feared. "But I assure you, you now have my undivided attention."

The younger woman actually preened. "We were discussing the Prince Regent," she cooed, widening her eyes in a most frightening manner. "Mama said he is looking for a new *friend*. And I said that it is shameful."

"The Prince Regent is not shameful," Worthington remarked, giving her a hard look. He had enough trouble without offending Prinny. "And I seriously doubt that he would appreciate his subjects discussing his private affairs."

The mother took the hint and nodded, but the daughter ignored him and rushed on. "But milord, a grandmother! Can you imagine?"

Of course *he* could imagine, but could *she?* From her expression, one would have thought Prinny was contemplating something really vile. Worthington considered how he might tell this child that her prurient imagination was running wild. At his present size, the Prince Regent was hardly fit for much physical exertion. No wonder he preferred older women. Prince or no prince, a man who had to be hoisted onto his horse with a pulley was not going to cut much of a swath with young and pretty ladies.

Lizzie caught his eye and smiled. "I should imagine that even grandmothers may have feelings," she said. "Feelings of love. Of respect."

"For the Prince Regent?" Miss Linden asked, in such obvious surprise that Worthington almost laughed.

"For the Prince Regent," Worthington declared. "But really, I meant what I said. The Prince Regent may conduct his life in any fashion he pleases. He is —"

"But the law —" Miss Linden began.

"The Prince is beyond the law." Worthington was determined to change the subject. "Come now, surely you ladies have done something of real interest lately."

Lady Linden's smile told him he had blundered — had, in fact, walked right into her trap.

"We visited Bullock's Egyptian Hall." She turned to Lizzie. "Such a magnificent place. I don't see how you can hope to compete with its attractions."

He waited for the signs. He knew when Lizzie's temper was rising — the tapping foot, the spark in her eye. But much to his surprise, her smile remained stationary. And sweet.

"Yes," she agreed. "It is a marvelous place. But we shall manage. There are many wonders in the world. Bullock's doesn't have them all."

"Oh, but they have so many," Miss Linden cried. "Why, there's a giant snake — thirty-five feet long! They call it a boa, boa —"

"Boa constrictor," said Lizzie, probably wishing it had decided to devour this particularly unpleasant person.

"I myself prefer the scene from the tropical rainforest," Lady Linden remarked, with a cloying smile at him. "The Indian hut is by far the most romantic thing I've ever seen."

With a look to Lizzie, Caroline said, "I

prefer the mother-of-pearl Chinese pagoda."

Lizzie nodded. Watching her, Worthington had the strangest notion that she was about to say something she shouldn't. That glint had come into her eye —

"Bullock's does not have what I shall have," Lizzie declared.

Miss Linden's eyes grew as large as meat pies, and her thin nose actually quivered in anticipation. "Oh, what? Do tell us."

Oh no! Lizzie couldn't mean to — He'd hoped for a little respite in the gossip. But if she — He cast her a look of appeal.

But she merely smiled. "My museum," she said proudly, her face aglow, "is going to have a learned pig."

For a moment both Lindens were rendered speechless. But only for a moment. Then the younger murmured, "A — a pig?"

"Precisely," said Lizzie. "But what a pig. He can spell, count, tell time."

"But —" sputtered Lady Linden. "A *pig!* Pigs are so utterly —"

"This one is actually quite clean," Lizzie said. "And quite intelligent. I have seen him perform, and he can actually do all that is claimed of him."

Lady Linden digested this in silence for

the space of one minute. Then, her eyes turned crafty. "Oh, dear," she cried. "I had quite forgot." She struggled to her feet, her various folds of fat undulating, her expression one of considerable agitation. "We must go immediately."

"But Mama —"

"We must go," the mother repeated. "I have an important appointment which had quite slipped my mind."

"Of course," Worthington said, trying not to sound too eager. "Do call again."

The Lindens exited in record time. "Well," he turned to Lizzie as the sound of the departing carriage reached them. "That was hardly politic. You realize, of course, why they left in such a hurry."

"I don't care," declared Caroline. "I am just grateful they left. Of all the callers we've had, those two are the very worst."

"They left," said Lizzie in answer to his statement, "to spread the news about Toby."

"Of course," cried Caroline, clapping her hands. "Oh, Elizabeth, you are brilliant!"

He shook his head. Females. "Your logic escapes me. By this time tomorrow, Bullock and everyone else in the city will know what you plan to do."

"Precisely," said Caroline with a giggle.

"Elizabeth has used the Lindens to get free advertisement for her museum."

"But —" He stopped. My word, the chit was right. He found himself grinning, his early good humor completely restored. "Amazing," he remarked, "you have succeeded in putting to good use two of the city's most useless inhabitants. My felicitations on your quick thinking."

She gave him a smile that would melt an ordinary man's bones. His own felt a little spongy. "Thank you, Worthington," she said. "Papa always said he admired my intelligence. But I thought he was just being kind."

"Oh, no," Worthington told her. "Your papa was quite accurate. You have very good intelligence. A shame, too."

Lizzie's foot began to tap. "A shame?" she cried, glaring at him. "What do you mean by that?"

When would he learn to think before he spoke? It wasn't like the old days, when he could tell her anything he pleased. He tried to explain. "I only meant that intelligence will not help you. Indeed, it may well prevent the gypsy's prophecy from being fulfilled. Most men prefer beauty to intelligence, you know."

"But Elizabeth has both," Caroline insisted.

90

"Yes, but you see, she doesn't hide her intelligence. And many men would be put off by it."

"But that is so unfair," Caroline declared, glaring at him. "So very unfair."

"Yes," Lizzie said, "it is. But he's right."

"But Elizabeth —"

Lizzie shook her head. "The world is as it is," she declared. "There is little point in our pretending otherwise." She gave him a strange look. "But your brother is forgetting something. Or perhaps I neglected to tell him the whole prophecy. Madame Nuranova said my husband would *love* me. That means he will take me as I am."

And, thought Worthington, the lucky man will soon be driven to distraction.

Elizabeth shifted in her chair. This talk of love was rather disconcerting, especially as she was acutely aware of Caroline's earlier declaration. Whomever Caroline loved, it could not be someone Worthington would approve. Otherwise, none of this secrecy would be necessary.

"Well," Worthington said with a sigh. "At least those two are gone."

"Yes," said Caroline. "Thank goodness for that."

Elizabeth cast about in her mind for a topic of conversation. With Worthington there, she could not pursue the real reason for her call. He seemed not to have heard all that Caroline had said as he was entering, but she certainly didn't want to arouse his suspicions.

"So," he said, in that cheerful tone he'd been using all day. "Have you made any more acquisitions for your museum?"

"A few, Worthington. But minor ones." That was it. The perfect, safe subject. "I have heard of another possibility, though."

"Yes?"

She hated to disturb his pleasant mood, but Caroline still looked very pale. A distraction was definitely called for. "I heard about a pig-faced lady —"

As she had hoped, he immediately straightened and prepared for battle. "Do you intend to make this a porcine museum?" he asked.

She couldn't help smiling. "No, indeed. It's just, well, the lady appears to be genuinely pig-faced."

"What a misfortune," cried Caroline. "The poor thing."

Worthington frowned. "I take it you haven't actually seen her."

"Oh no. She's in Sussex. That seems a long trip."

He raised an eyebrow, but he merely said,

"When do you wish to leave?"

He asked so pleasantly that for a moment she was at a loss. "I — I do not know. Actually, I had thought —"

His smile was brilliant — and a trifle mocking. "That I would try to dissuade you? Oh no, Lizzie. I gave you my word. And I mean to keep it. So, when shall we depart for Sussex?"

Caroline's mouth hung open. Whether her shock had been initiated by his attitude or by the use of the nickname, Elizabeth could not tell. She tried to pull herself together. "I — I do not — that is, I don't think it kind to use the lady's misfortunes. To be put on display in such a vulgar way must be quite distressing to the poor creature."

Now, now he would turn irritable and stomp out. But to her surprise, he merely smiled. "You're quite right, Lizzie. That admirable intelligence of yours has won out again. So it seems we shall forgo a trip to Sussex." And he settled back into his chair with a complacent smile.

Chapter Six

Two days later, days in which Elizabeth had still not had a chance to discover the name of the man Caroline loved, Barton interrupted her afternoon's work to announce, "The Marquis of Worthington and his sister, milady."

Elizabeth sighed, but she said, "Show them right in." She looked around the room. Many of the items had already been moved to their museum displays, but others were still clustered here and there. And she had still so much to do.

Now, where was that dog? She whistled. "Fufu, *come.*"

The little dog emerged from under a chair and had just about reached her side when Worthington appeared in the doorway. Fufu set up a yapping that would have done credit to a far larger animal and lunged expertly for Worthington's ankles.

Fortunately, he was wearing his polished Hessians. Otherwise, the dog's teeth would have bit to the bone. *"Fufu! Stop that!"* Elizabeth called in exasperation. "Come here this minute!"

With one last yip, the dog retreated to a far corner, where he contented himself with an occasional low growl.

"I'm sorry," Elizabeth told her guests. "He gets a little overprotective sometimes. Do come in. Find a place to sit — if you can. Caroline, how nice to see you."

The two found chairs. Worthington settled into his with a sigh that indicated a perturbed state of mind. "That creature is a menace," he said, frowning at the dog. From his corner, the dog, as though understanding him, growled.

Poor Fufu . . . he was no match for Tom-Tom. Elizabeth managed a smile. "He's just doing his job. So, what news do you bring me today?"

Caroline flushed and Worthington scowled, but neither replied. "Whatever is wrong?" Elizabeth asked, glancing from one to the other. "You look as though you'd lost your last friend."

"No." Caroline hesitated. "It's not us. It's just that — well, Lady Linden came to call."

Elizabeth chuckled. "No wonder you look so poorly."

Worthington's scowl deepened. "What my sister is trying to tell you is —"

"We are bringing bad news." Caroline

sighed. "And we do not quite know how to tell you."

Elizabeth controlled her exasperation. "Well, just spit it out. For heaven's sake, do you want to frighten me half to death?"

"Oh no," Caroline continued. "We don't wish to do that. It's just that —"

"Bullock's has engaged a learned pig." Worthington had leaned forward in his chair and was watching her closely.

"He has *what?*"

"It's true," Caroline cried. "Everyone is talking about it. And, and he's engaged it for the same week, the week your museum opens."

Damnation! Why had she had to shoot off her mouth in front of those blabbering Lindens? "Are you quite sure of this?"

Worthington nodded. "Quite sure. He's already begun advertising." He gave her a rueful look. "I am sorry, Lizzie. I know the museum means a lot to you."

This magnanimity of his rather staggered her. Why hadn't he laughed and said I told you so?

Well, she certainly could behave as well as he could. She mustered a smile. "It's my own fault. For wanting to impress that — that — well, we shall just have to add another attraction. Something even more startling."

His eyebrow shot up. "And what might that be?"

"I'm not sure. I shall have to think on it."

A strange expression crossed Caroline's face. "You know, Lizzie —" She stopped and flushed. "I'm sorry. I shouldn't presume. But Worthington calls you that so often I am coming to think of you in that way."

Elizabeth managed another smile. Her politeness was certainly being strained this day. "It's all right, Caroline. Though I would prefer that no one else hear it."

"Of course. Well, there is something I've been wanting very much to see. And I think perhaps others would enjoy it, too."

Worthington gave his sister an amused look. "Come now, Caroline, Lizzie can't very well put that poet fellow on display in her place. What's his name? Shelley? People won't pay hard cash to see that kind of fellow."

Caroline made a face at him. "You are just jealous. Mr. Shelley is an excellent poet. He has much to say. But I wasn't thinking about Lizzie exhibiting him."

"Then what *were* you thinking?" Elizabeth asked.

Caroline straightened in her chair. "I know it sounds foolish, but I have always wanted to see a sword-swallower perform."

Worthington almost leaped to his feet. "A what?"

Caroline ignored him. "Or a fire-eater. Both would draw crowds, I'm sure."

Elizabeth found the look of utter dismay on Worthington's face almost worth the disruption of her afternoon's work. "That's an excellent idea, Caroline. I shall set about finding one immediately."

Worthington arranged his features into a semblance of calm, but she knew from that little twitch in his cheek that he was not nearly as composed as he looked. "Might I suggest," he said dryly, "that the sword-swallower seems the safer choice? He, at least, cannot burn the building down."

Elizabeth suppressed her smile. "You're quite right, Worthington." She looked around her. "Now, if you'll forgive me, I have —"

Caroline sent her a strange look, almost pleading. "I asked Worthington to leave me here for a while. While he makes some other calls. I'm not feeling quite up to snuff, but I did want to be here when you found out about Bullock's pig! Oh, Lizzie, how can you remain so calm? You are so strong . . . so wonderful."

Elizabeth was not feeling wonderful.

Indeed, she was feeling quite harassed. There was still a great deal of work to do before opening day. And now she must arrange yet another journey and spend this afternoon, which she sorely needed for other things, helping Caroline with her problem.

It was not that she didn't care for her friend. Or that she was not willing to help. But everything seemed to be pressing in on her. Still, Caroline was obviously in need of a friendly ear.

"Of course," Elizabeth said, looking to Worthington. "Just leave her here till you're finished."

Worthington got to his feet, sent the dog a dark threatening look, and made his way to the door. "I shall save Monday next for our sword-swallowing trip, then. Till later."

They waited some minutes after he had gone, sitting in a heavy silence. Then Elizabeth said, "I think it's safe to talk now."

Caroline nodded. "Yes, he must be gone. But I — I don't know where to begin."

"Begin with this man's name," Elizabeth said, trying to control her impatience. "Who is he?"

Caroline looked down at her hands. "I — I'm afraid to tell you."

This could not go on. With so much to do she could not play guessing games. "Caroline! It's not that poet! That Shelley?"

Caroline giggled. "Mercy, no. It's — it's James Mitchell."

Elizabeth heaved a sigh of relief. "Your brother's steward?"

"Yes. Oh, Lizzie, do remember what you said."

Elizabeth put her hands to her throbbing head. Worthington was not going to like this. "What I said about what?" she asked.

"About marrying a coachman."

Worthington's sister *would* remember that. "Oh, that."

"Lizzie!"

"Caroline, for mercy's sake. Do be quiet and let me think for a minute."

Caroline subsided into silence and Elizabeth's thoughts raced. Finally she asked, "Does your brother have any idea that you have formed this affection for James Mitchell?"

"I think not. Else he would have exploded."

Elizabeth nodded. Worthington was not the sort to seethe in silence.

"Now, has James — does he — That is —" Elizabeth found the subject difficult to broach. "What I'm trying to say is, how does he feel about you?"

Caroline smiled. "I don't know. It isn't

like that other time." She blushed deeply. "He has not said anything. He's a good man, Lizzie. He thinks himself beneath me. He would not do anything to hurt me."

"Well, that's a relief."

"Yes, but — how am I to manage it?"

Elizabeth sighed. This love business was such a tangle. But at least Mitchell was a decent man, not like that other one.

"You'll speak to him, won't you?" Caroline pleaded.

"I? Your brother won't listen to me."

Caroline paled. "Not to Worthington, Lizzie. To James."

Elizabeth stared at her friend. "You want me to persuade Mitchell to ask for you? Why, your brother would have my head!"

"But Lizzie, there's no other way."

"Of course there is. We must get Worthington to think it is *his* idea."

Caroline's eyes widened. "But how?"

"Let me think on it."

"You know how he is." Caroline worried her lower lip with her teeth. "He's so set, so determined. He means for me to wed Vidon, you know."

"I shouldn't worry about that." Elizabeth smiled. "The viscount calls on Sarah nearly every day."

"But still —"

"Hush, now! I'm getting a glimmer of an idea."

Obediently Caroline became silent.

Finally Elizabeth nodded. "I think I may have a plan. But it will be difficult. You will need to be strong, to persevere."

"Oh, I'll do anything. I just want to marry James."

Elizabeth bent closer. "Well, then, here is what we shall do."

Monday next proved to be a lovely day for a drive into the country. Elizabeth, who shared a seat with Sarah and Nanny, found herself looking often at Worthington, who was seated across from her. His habit of clutching at his shoulder had more than once made her wonder if some permanent damage had been done him in the fighting. But Caroline had assured her that he was quite fit. So perhaps it was just a habit he had fallen into.

At any rate, he was clearly not his old self. He'd been staring out at the countryside for the entire journey and remained quite morose.

On the other hand, Viscount Vidon was in the most cheerful of moods, laughing and chatting with Sarah until her face fairly glowed.

Elizabeth swallowed a sigh. Thank goodness Vidon was a man of honor. Madame Nuranova's prediction for Sarah seemed more and more likely to come true. But from the scowls that he occasionally sent in his friend's direction, Worthington was clearly not in favor of such a liaison.

"Can't see why you've got to do this kind of thing," Nanny complained. "All this gallivanting about is hard on old bones."

In her present mood Elizabeth had scant pity for the old woman. "Then you should have stayed home. We are quite safe."

"Safe from highwaymen, mayhap." Nanny's tone turned grim. "But there's plenty other dangers in this world."

Unaccountably, Elizabeth found herself looking at Worthington. He did not seem insulted, but she flushed anyway. "Surely, Nanny, you don't think we are in any danger from —"

"Didn't say *him*," Nanny returned.

"It's the gossips she's thinking of," Worthington observed. "And she's quite correct. You must have a care for your reputation."

Though she was sorely tempted to argue just for the sake of prolonging the conversation, she knew Nanny was right. Actually, they were both right. One could not be too careful.

She met Worthington's eyes again, but they were veiled, keeping her out. Once, in those faraway days, he'd been her friend, the best friend she'd ever had. If only she could bring those days back. She leaned forward. "Do you remember the time you let me ride your pony?"

He nodded, his mouth twisting in a wry grin. "Yes, indeed. He threw you off and ran away. I had the devil's own time catching him. And I got a dressing down from my father, to boot." He sighed dramatically. "You were a deal of trouble."

"We did have fun, though."

He raised an eyebrow. "Fun? You call finding a spider in your bread and butter *fun?*"

She shrugged and bit back a smile. "Just because a spider strayed —"

He leaned forward, his expression severe. "The spider did not *stray*. That spider was deliberately —"

"Why, I should never —"

"Oh yes, you did," Nanny interrupted grimly. "Always wanted your own way. Usually got it, too. And now look at you."

Worthington, watching this exchange with more interest than he had felt all day, saw Lizzie color up.

"I don't think I am doing anything wrong, Nanny. This museum was Papa's wish." She cast Worthington a glance. "His dying wish."

Nanny sighed. "Still, you could have set someone else to do the work. It ain't decent for a lady to go grubbing about old bones and things."

Lizzie frowned. "I am not *grubbing about.* I am doing scientific work."

Worthington swallowed his dry remark. Lizzie was getting miffed. Her foot was tapping and the fire had begun to blaze in her eyes.

Nanny heaved a sigh of tremendous melancholy. "Important work is getting a husband. That's the only work a decent young woman ought to be about. Getting herself a husband. A good one."

Now, Nanny had the right idea there. What Lizzie needed was a man, someone to take her in hand. He ran over a mental list of all the suitable men he knew, but it was a useless task. Lizzie would eat any of those fellows for breakfast. What she needed was someone stronger than she was. Smarter. Richer.

Someone — the thought almost made him start in alarm from his carriage seat, but he calmed himself. Even if he offered for her, Lizzie would not have him. Too bad, in a way . . . life with her would certainly be interesting. Of course, he had no intention of getting leg-shackled — at least, not for some time. And certainly not to someone who put spiders in his bread and butter.

While he was considering this, they arrived at the village. Vidon popped out of the carriage first, irritatingly cheerful, and helped the ladies down.

Elizabeth, following Vidon out of the carriage, wished herself at home in her study. She was increasingly uncomfortable in the presence of Worthington and she was not really sure why. Perhaps it was this longing to return to the simple friendship of the old days, a longing which he obviously didn't share. Perhaps it was her awareness of Sarah's growing attachment to the viscount — and his to her — of which she knew Worthington disapproved. Or perhaps, she told herself as he offered her his arm, perhaps it was because she was conspiring with his sister to set up an alliance she knew quite well he would be dead set against.

None of this thinking made her any more comfortable, and as they entered the Inn of the Two Boars, where the sword swallower had agreed to meet them, she pushed such thoughts aside.

A plump little man, almost as round as he was tall, rose from his seat and smiled at her. "Ah, signora, I am pleased to meet you. I understand you have need for a man of my talents."

"Yes, Madame Nuranova said —"

"She is right. I — Pietro Cavelli — I am the world's greatest swallower of swords. I swallow two, three, four — all at once."

Worthington sighed, a sigh so huge she felt it in the arm she leaned on. "And how do you do that?" he asked.

Signor Cavelli's round face registered utter amazement. "This I cannot say. This, this is secret, handed down from my father's father's father. Of this we do not speak."

The little man looked so perturbed that Elizabeth moved to soothe him. "Of course not, Signor Cavelli. You must forgive his lordship. He has a strange sense of humor."

Signor Cavelli nodded. "These English I do not always understand. Madame Nuranova tells me you open a museum. In London. And there you want me to perform."

Elizabeth nodded. "That's right. The museum is opening the first week in September. Can you —"

Worthington's insistent pulling at her arm stopped her in mid-sentence. "Excuse me a moment, Signor Cavelli." She turned to Worthington. "Yes, what is it?"

He leaned toward her and whispered, "I don't mean to interfere, but shouldn't you see the man perform before you engage him?" His lips were so close she felt his warm breath on her ear, and the strangest sensation slipped over her body, ending with a weakness in her knees.

And then his words registered. There he was again, telling her what to do. Common sense, of course, told her he was right. But he simply had to learn that she could handle things on her own.

She turned back to the little Italian. "Now, Signor Cavelli, as I was saying . . ." And she went ahead and engaged the man without having seen any evidence of his skills.

She contemplated this rather foolish behavior on the ride home, a ride which seemed to last for ages. Nanny complained of everything from the weather, which was actually the best part of the day, to the seat on which they sat, which was certainly no harder than any seat in any carriage in England.

Sarah, of course, did not complain. She

and Vidon, oblivious to all else, sat gazing at each other with enchanted eyes. Elizabeth found this only made her discontent more manifest, especially as Worthington insisted on sitting wordlessly, staring out the window like a man made of stone.

Several times she considered trying to open a conversation with him. But he was so plainly put out with her that she remained silent.

Well, this trip would end eventually and he would get over his disgruntlement with her. So, she had made a slight error of judgment in telling the Lindens about the learned pig. Still, she was perfectly capable of handling her own affairs. Why couldn't the man see that?

Chapter Seven

August became September. Working every day and long into the night, Elizabeth finally had everything displayed to her liking. Mr. Elderby, hired as ticket taker and general factotum, was a great help.

Toby and Mr. Ware took up residence in the back room of the museum. Toby, it seemed, was housebroken, and indeed, of the two, Mr. Ware appeared to offer more cause for concern. Given his amazing capacity for gin, he might perhaps have been a show in himself.

Signor Cavelli also arrived, complete with a theatrical-looking costume of red velvet and a case of assorted sharp instruments for swallowing. Fortunately, he made his residence in a nearby inn and not in the museum itself.

The morning of the museum opening dawned bright and clear. Elizabeth, pacing the floor nervously till Worthington arrived to pick her up, tried to calm her nerves, but she found herself inordinately glad that Worthington had insisted that he and Caroline accompany her to the museum.

When he helped the ladies down from the carriage outside the front door, it was still lacking half an hour till opening time. "No one is here!" Elizabeth exclaimed. "I knew no one would come."

Worthington frowned. "Come, come, Lizzie. Brace up under fire, now. Don't turn yellow on me." He squeezed her arm. "There's plenty of time yet. Let's go inside and get you a cup of tea. You need calming."

She allowed him to lead her inside. He was being very kind to her. And she was planning to —

"This animal!" yelled Signor Cavelli, leaping out from behind the door as it opened. "This pig! You do not tell me I perform with a pig! Such a disgrace."

Oh no, thought Elizabeth. If one more thing went wrong . . . "Come, Signor Cavelli," she soothed. "You are not performing *with* the pig. You are performing alone. In a different room. You are the best. It is *you* everyone will come to see."

But the little Italian would not be placated. Waving his hands wildly, he sputtered on about artistic integrity till she almost wished she could silence him with one of his own shining daggers.

Finally Worthington whispered. "Go see to Toby. I'll take care of this."

She nodded in relief and set out for the back room with Caroline at her heels. But halfway there she began to have second thoughts. Perhaps she should have refused Worthington's help. She could have handled this. Some way. But Worthington was there and he wanted to help. Wouldn't it have been rude to refuse him?

"Mr. Ware?" she called, knocking on the door. The man had to be ready on time. They had scheduled an early performance because of the opening. She knocked again, this time more insistently. "Mr. Ware?"

There was no answer. With a look at Caroline she eased open the door. "Oh no!"

Toby lay in his bed of straw — 600 pounds of clean pink pig, fast asleep, and snoring to boot. And beside him, his arm thrown companionably over the hog's back, and considerably less clean, lay a disheveled Mr. Ware, also snoring.

Elizabeth crossed the room toward him, but halfway there she was assailed by the stench of gin. "Mr. Ware!" she cried. "Wake up! It's almost time for your performance!"

The pig opened one eye and grunted. The master did not even twitch.

"Do you think," Caroline asked, "that the

pig has been imbibing, too?"

"Let us hope not," Worthington observed from the doorway. "Usually animals have more sense."

Elizabeth did not turn to look at him. If he dared to laugh at her . . . She had never felt more like screaming. Why must everything go wrong? And just when she was trying to prove to Worthington that she was capable of handling this place on her own. "Mr. Ware!" She bent to shake him, a distasteful task at best, now made more disgusting by the stench of stale alcohol that hovered in his vicinity.

"I'd advise a bucket of cold water," Worthington said. "I'll get it."

"But Signor Cavelli —"

"I've attended to him. He will be all right." And he went off to fetch the water.

Elizabeth sighed. "I must have been out of my mind," she said, half to herself, "to even have thought of engaging such an attraction."

The pig made several settling-to-sleep noises and then commenced to snore again. Behind her Elizabeth heard another strange sound. She turned and saw Caroline, vainly struggling to stifle her laughter with a handkerchief held to her mouth. When she found herself discovered, she hurried to say, "Oh

Elizabeth, I am sorry. But — but the picture they present. It is so — so amusing."

In spite of herself Elizabeth had to agree. "You're right. They look like —"

"Like brothers!" Caroline broke into laughter. "Exactly like brothers!"

And that was how Worthington found them when he returned, clutching each other and laughing uproariously while the pig and his master slept peacefully on.

Half an hour later, Mr. Ware was on his feet, slightly wobbly and more than a little damp. But at least he was mobile.

Elizabeth, making a tour of the museum's rooms on Worthington's arm, said, "Thank you. I don't know if I could have managed Mr. Ware myself."

"You're welcome." Worthington actually smiled at her. "I'm enjoying myself." He looked over her shoulder and his smile slowly changed quality. "At least I *was*. Here come Lady Linden and that mercenary daughter of hers."

Elizabeth summoned a smile of her own. She had no intention of letting either Linden suspect anything had gone amiss.

"Oh Lady Elizabeth! How nice to see you," Lady Linden gushed in her usual false tones.

114

"I'm pleased you were able to come to our opening," Elizabeth returned. Actually, that was a bold-faced lie. She would have been quite happy never to lay eyes on this scandal-mongering pair again. But politeness dictated a certain degree of civility.

"I am particularly eager to see the sword-swallower," Miss Linden confided with a wide-eyed glance at Worthington. "He sounds so romantic."

Since Elizabeth could think of nothing less romantic than the rotund Signor Cavelli, she found this rather difficult to respond to. Evidently so did Tom-Tom, for he remained silent.

Miss Linden gazed up at him in adoration. "Have you seen the pig at Bullock's?" she inquired.

Worthington shook his head. "No, I'm afraid not. I reserve all my patronage for Lady Elizabeth's museum."

"He's really an intelligent pig." Miss Linden chattered on, declaiming on the marvelous pig and his antics until Elizabeth found herself grinding her teeth in frustration.

Just when she thought she could bear no more, the chiming of a bell called all the patrons to the center of the largest room, where provisions had been made for Toby to perform. Elizabeth followed the Lindens there, while Worthington and Caroline went to check again on Signor Cavelli.

Mr. Ware, still looking a little green around the gills, waited till the crowd had collected. "Ladies and gentlemen," he cried, standing with his feet planted wide as though the floor might suddenly move on him. "Let me present Toby, the smartest pig in all of England!"

"There's a smarter pig at Bullock's," Miss Linden cried.

Mr. Ware looked first amazed, and then hurt. "How can you be saying such a thing? Why, Toby'll be having his feelings hurt most dreadful!"

The pig gave a heartrending squeal and rolled his eyes.

"Now see what you've gone and done!" cried Mr. Ware, as Toby attempted to hide his massive head between his front legs.

Elizabeth held back a smile. Mr. Ware had obviously been heckled before and had developed a routine to deal with it. But poor Miss Linden did not know this and had turned scarlet.

"Now, now, Toby." Mr. Ware patted the pig's head. "The lady didn't mean nothing by it. She'll apologize. Won't you, miss?"

Obviously Miss Linden didn't know how

116

to respond. She looked to her mama, but that lady seemed equally nonplussed by recent events.

"You've got to say you're sorry, miss. Else he won't do nothing more." Mr. Ware looked out over the crowd. "And all these good folks what come to see him'll be mighty disappointed."

Mutters ran through the crowd and people turned to gaze on Miss Linden with looks that were far from friendly.

"You just tell him you're sorry, miss. And he'll go right on. He'll even tell the time for you, he will."

Miss Linden's face was still scarlet, but the murmurs of those around her were apparently more convincing than her convictions about Toby's intelligence. "I — I am sorry," she stammered. And the pig raised his head, nodding vigorously, and squealed again, though this time more happily.

"Now," said Mr. Ware, "if the lady has a timepiece, or one of you gents, Toby'll tell you the correct time."

Elizabeth moved slowly toward the back of the crowd. Mr. Ware appeared to have suffered no lasting ill effects from his over-indulgence in gin. Indeed, his wits were as sharp as ever. And Toby was his usual erudite self.

She had intended to speak to the master severely. Behavior like his recent drunkenness could not be condoned. But she had to admit that his handling of Miss Linden's challenge had been superb. Perhaps his misbehavior could be overlooked this once. But he must not let it happen again.

When Toby began carrying the cards that spelled out his name, she allowed herself a sigh of relief. Perhaps the museum opening would get off without a mishap after all. At least Toby was doing —

An insistent pull at her arm made her turn. "Worthington says to come," Caroline whispered. "Signor Cavelli —"

Elizabeth waited to hear no more, but, avoiding the Lindens, hurried to the room set aside for the display of weapons. The little Italian perched morosely on a great rock meant to represent the Scottish highlands. In his red velvet suit he looked monstrously out of place. Beside him, Worthington glowered, a picture of lordly outrage.

"Signor Cavelli," she asked in consternation, "whatever is wrong?"

His whole body quivered with his anger, a sight that under other circumstances she might have found amusing. "This pig!" he cried. "He has unnerve me. I — I am the

118

Great Cavelli. And you ask me — me! — to share billing with a pig! This — this wounds me. I cannot perform. Is not right."

Though in her present mood she would have preferred to throttle him, Elizabeth put on her sweetest most soothing smile. "Signor Cavelli, I am sorry. But think of the wonderful opportunity here. You have the chance to show your — your art to many people."

The little Italian shook his head, his moustache twitching in agitation. "These — these *canaille,* they know nothing of art."

She used her ultimate argument. "Then you must teach them."

He struck himself dramatically on the chest. "I — I cannot work where a pig works. Is — is —"

While the sword swallower struggled for the right words, Worthington spoke. "Then perhaps you'd better leave."

"But —" The pressure of his hand on her arm silenced Elizabeth. Well, then, let Tom-Tom try. He would be no more successful than she had been in dealing with this irritating little man.

"Leave?" cried the sword-swallower. "Yes, I leave. You give me my money. I leave."

Worthington's face turned hard. "Money? You have no money coming."

"My fee —"

Worthington looked coldly down his nose. "Your fee was for performing. You have not performed."

"I tell you! The pig — he upsets me!"

Worthington shook his head. "Tough luck, old fellow. No performance, no money."

The Italian looked pleadingly to Elizabeth. She was tempted to double his fee if he would consent to perform. But she could just see Worthington's reaction to that! And besides, for once, Tom-Tom was right. The man had been engaged to perform. Now let him do it.

When she didn't respond, Signor Cavelli sighed heavily. "Is on *your* head," he said. "Is not my fault if things go wrong."

Worthington consulted his timepiece. "In ten minutes, then, we'll expect a performance." And he led Elizabeth away.

Surely, she thought, as they moved through the crowd, through the rooms of displays, surely Papa had not had this much difficulty dealing with people. She risked a glance at Worthington. Probably, without his help, Mr. Ware would still be lying in a drunken stupor. And the sword-swallower would already have been gone. Life had not prepared her for dealing with such types. But Tom-Tom had known exactly what to do.

For the first time she faced the fact that she had been wrong about something. She had underestimated her ability to deal with these people. Nanny and Elias and the others were loyal retainers, people who had been with her all her life. When she told them she wanted something done, it was done. But now she was seeing that dealing with outsiders was quite different. And quite exhausting.

The chimes sounded at the appointed hour and Worthington led her back toward the weapons room where Signor Cavelli was to perform. "Don't worry," Tom-Tom said, patting her hand. "I know his kind. He will do it."

She sincerely hoped so. For it had just occurred to her that perhaps Signor Cavelli's distress was manufactured to hide the fact that he could not do what he had been engaged to do. Oh Lord, how Tom-Tom would carry on if that should be true! She could just see the expression of disdain on his face as he said, "I told you so."

Signor Cavelli stood upon the improvised stage, dressed in his resplendent red velvet and looking like an overgrown ripe apple. On the table beside him, spread out on a black cloth, glittered an assortment of swords and daggers, a truly magnificent sight. And all around him clustered the curious, Miss Linden and her mama prominently placed in the forefront.

"I show you," Signor Cavelli began. "I show you how a man may swallow many swords."

If only he would dispense with the bombast, Elizabeth thought, as he rattled on and on, and get to the show. When finally the first sword disappeared down his throat, she let out a sigh of relief rather louder than it should have been. Worthington turned to her, his expression quizzical. "Nanny is right, you know. You should hire someone to manage this place for you."

She bristled. She couldn't help it. Just because he'd given her a little assistance, he thought he had the right to tell her what to do! "I can manage quite well," she said, striving for an even tone. "Of course I expected a few mishaps." His expression of disbelief made her pause momentarily. She wanted to be fair. "I do thank you for your help today. But I should have managed without it — some way or other."

Worthington had the common sense to

keep his tongue between his teeth. Now was not the time to tell her she was wrong, that running this place would take a great deal of energy and perhaps more knowledge of common people than she possessed. He'd be willing to bet a pretty sum that until this morning she'd never even seen a man in his cups, let alone had to wake one who'd over-indulged in gin. And as for the little Italian — a knowledgeable person expected temperament in his kind. Hadn't the great Catalani thrown a fit of temper and threatened to walk out of the opera house in the middle of a concert? And that more than once?

Yes, it was a good thing Lizzie had *him*. A good thing he was looking out for her. And he would continue to do so, no matter how ungrateful she appeared. He smiled. For the first time in months he was actually enjoying himself. And it was all due to Lizzie's wonderful folly of a museum.

Chapter Eight

Two days later an exhausted Elizabeth sipped her breakfast tea and read the paper. Then, frowning, she threw the *Morning Chronicle* down. When Signor Cavelli saw this, he was going to explode.

Then, fighting a smile, she picked it up again. The caricature in the style of Gillray portrayed Toby standing upright, ready to swallow a dagger — and Signor Cavelli, on all fours, preparing to push a lettered card with his nose. "Which is which?" the caption asked.

It truly was funny. But of course, the sword-swallower could not be expected to see the humor in it. She would be lucky if he finished out his week. She sighed. Now she'd have to find another attraction. She picked up a quill. Perhaps Madame Nuranova could suggest someone — someone not so temperamental.

Caroline arrived while she was still writing. "Have you seen the *Morning Chronicle*?"

"Of course. A great likeness, don't you think?"

Caroline giggled. "Of Signor Cavelli, or of Toby?"

"Both. So what brings you here?"

Caroline sobered. "Our plan. Our plan will not work without a suitable object. And so far we have found none."

Elizabeth sighed. "You're quite right. I hadn't supposed it would be quite so difficult a task."

"Nor I," Caroline agreed.

Elizabeth looked at her friend. "I am writing to Madame Nuranova — to find me a fire-eater. When we go to see him, why don't you come along? You'll like the gypsy camp."

It took several days for a reply to come back from the gypsy queen. Immediately Elizabeth sent Worthington a message and, true to his word, he arranged for the journey. And so the end of the week they arrived at Madame Nuranova's new camp. Very much like the previous one, it nestled in a little meadow surrounded by trees. The benders and tents were a bright display of color, covered with blankets and felts of many hues.

Caroline looked around wide-eyed. "Oh Elizabeth, how very romantic!"

Her brother gave her a dark look and Elizabeth swallowed a sigh. The man meant well. But he couldn't seem to understand that a young girl had dreams.

She herself, though no longer so young, dreamt of a husband and little ones. It was a dream she mentioned to no one, least of all Nanny, who would have crowed triumphantly.

It was not, Elizabeth told herself, that she didn't want a husband, only that she wanted one she could love. She knew love was a luxury few women could afford. But nevertheless she was determined not to marry unless she could have it. She wanted a man she could love, a man she could respect . . . one who could be depended upon to handle things — like the mishaps at the museum.

Tom-Tom had done that, of course. And she knew she could depend on him. But it was not the same. He was her friend. Now, if he were her husband —

There was no time to consider this startling thought, however, for Madame Nuranova was coming across the meadow toward her. "You are welcome," she said, smiling at them.

Elizabeth returned the smile. "You have met the marquis."

The gypsy queen nodded gravely. "The

126

brave man. The man with anger. You are welcome, Elizabeth's friend."

Elizabeth turned to Caroline. "And this is his sister. Caroline, this is Madame Nuranova, the queen of the gypsies."

Caroline's face flushed with color. "Madame Nuranova, I am so pleased to meet you. What a lovely campsite you have here!"

The gypsy nodded. "We are happy. We have trees. We have sun. We have air."

Worthington cleared his throat and frowned. The gypsy smiled enigmatically. "This one cares not for beauty?"

Worthington had the grace to look slightly uncomfortable. "He was wounded," Elizabeth explained. "In the war. And he —"

"And the heart still pains." Madame Nuranova nodded sagely. "It will heal," she said, giving Elizabeth a strange glance from her dark eyes. "Love heals all."

Elizabeth's heart rose up in her throat. Could Madame Nuranova mean that she — But how could she love Tom-Tom?

"The fire-eater waits," the gypsy said.

Elizabeth pulled herself together. She must stop thinking about husbands and love and think about the museum. "Of course."

Caroline came up beside her to whisper, "Why did she look at you like that?"

"I — I don't know. Come, we must see the fire-eater."

Madame Nuranova led the way to the center of the meadow where a small fire burned. Elizabeth looked around, hopefully the fire-eater would be somewhat more romantic than Signor Cavelli.

"You sit here," Madame Nuranova said, indicating some cane chairs. "Soon she starts."

"She?" Caroline and Elizabeth repeated in chorus.

The gypsy nodded. "She is very good. Señorita Giaconda. Straight from Spain she comes. You watch."

A pretty little dark-haired woman came smiling into the circle. She tasted burning brands. She passed her hands through the flames. She walked barefoot over hot coals.

Elizabeth heard Worthington's sharp intake of breath. The fire-eater was truly amazing. There was no trickery here. The flames were quite real, and so were the coals.

"It's the most astounding thing," Caroline cried. "How can she do it?"

For once Worthington didn't have anything to say.

"I don't know," Elizabeth replied. "But she is certainly very good."

Madame Nuranova nodded. "I knew you

would like. You wish to hire her?"

For some inexplicable reason Elizabeth found herself turning to Worthington. "What do you think?"

He looked quite startled, as well he might. Not only had she not asked his opinion before, she had ignored it when it was given. And now . . .

"I —" Plainly he was trying to gather his wits. "I think Señorita Giaconda is a rare find. I congratulate you on your friendship with Madame Nuranova."

Elizabeth nodded. She turned to the queen. "Thank you. I shall certainly engage her." She turned back to the performer. "Now, Señorita Giaconda —"

"She does not understand the English," said Madame Nuranova.

Worthington muttered, "I might have known."

But Elizabeth contented herself with a sigh. "I want her for the museum. But I don't speak Spanish. I can't hire —"

"There is no reason to worry." Madame Nuranova's throaty voice carried absolute conviction. "Her brother — he speaks the English."

"And he will come to London with her?" Elizabeth asked.

"But of course." Madame Nuranova

129

clapped and a tall dark-skinned man stepped out of the crowd. *"Buenos dias,"* he said. "You wish to hire my sister?"

"Yes," Elizabeth replied. She felt Caroline's fingers closing around her arm, and patted her hand. "Yes. I want her to perform in my museum."

The gypsy nodded. "We shall come. The queen says it is so. But we cannot stay many weeks. Too long in the city makes us ill."

"I understand." Again she found herself turning to Worthington. "What do you think? The same sum we pay Signor Cavelli?"

He nodded. "That seems fair. Perhaps a little more. Since there are two of them."

"Good." She turned back to the Spaniard and concluded the final details. "Then we shall expect you on Monday."

She looked at the sky. "It is getting late. We'll have to start back."

Madame Nuranova's dark eyes gleamed. "Why do you not stay? Tonight we have bonfire. Gypsy wedding. Big feast, much music. You will like."

Elizabeth found she very much wanted to stay, to feel — if only for a little while — free from the peering eyes of the *ton.* But there was Worthington to consider. "Oh, Madame Nuranova, I should like to. But

130

I'm afraid there are things —"

"I think we should stay." Worthington's words took her completely by surprise.

She stared at him. "You do?"

"Yes, I do."

With difficulty he kept himself from laughing at her amazed expression. Lizzie had never liked to be laughed at. No more than he. But he knew he had correctly interpreted that look of yearning on her face. She wanted very much to stay. And, if the truth must be told, he wouldn't mind sleeping under the stars again himself.

"But is it proper?" she asked.

Now it was his turn to stare. And this time he did laugh. "My dear Lizzie. When have you ever let anything like propriety stand in your way?"

She returned his smile, but she did not look convinced. "But to stay out here —"

"You have Caroline and Nanny. Surely that is chaperonage enough. Madame Nuranova will provide you with shelter. And I shall sleep under the stars."

The gypsy queen chuckled. "You make good gypsy." She turned to the women. "Come, I show you to tent. All for you. Wedding starts soon."

Lizzie looked at him again. Plainly she was still surprised. "If you're sure it's all right."

"Of course I'm sure." He watched the women trail after the gypsy to the tent. Strange, Lizzie asking *his* opinion. She'd never done a thing like that before.

As darkness fell, the gypsies gathered by the fire. In the interim, the men had set up huge tables and the women loaded them with food. The bonfire had been fed and grown larger.

"You sit here," Madame Nuranova said. "You are honored guests."

Worthington's curiosity finally got the better of him. "How did you get to be so honored?" he asked.

Lizzie's smile was complacent. "Because of Papa. He always allowed the gypsies to camp on our land. For as long as they liked." With a glance at Nanny, she lowered her voice. "I used to sneak off and play with the gypsy children."

He chuckled. "And did you lead them into the suds, as you did me?"

"No, I don't think so." Her forehead wrinkled into a frown. "Worthington?"

"Yes?"

"How is it that you remember so much trouble connected with me?"

He could see by her expression that she was uncomfortable in asking. "I don't know. What do you remember?"

She gave him a timid smile. "I remember fun. And having a friend. It was wonderful."

The poignancy of her tone caught him unawares. What could it mean? "Surely you had other friends?"

"Not like you. You were so strong. So brave. We shared so much. Remember when we talked about running away to become pirates?"

"Yes, I remember. I tried to tell you that only men could be pirates."

"And I told you about Anne Bonny." She sighed and her face went serious. "I have not had such a friend since."

"Nor I," he said, meaning merely to be polite, but discovering quite suddenly that what he said was true.

Tears gleamed in her eyes. "Why did growing up have to destroy that?"

Without thinking, he covered her gloved hand with his. "Perhaps it didn't have to," he said softly. "Perhaps we can have it again."

Her lower lip quivered slightly. He leaned forward a little and realized an appalling urge to take her in his arms. He straightened abruptly. Good Lord! He could not be developing a *tendre* for Lizzie.

And yet, what was so wrong with that?

True, she was headstrong. But she had been quite amenable lately. Of course, she would never really be tractable. Not Lizzie. And she would make a man's life into a bumble broth.

He leaned back in his chair. Still . . .

Elizabeth, looking at Caroline's wide eyes and flushed face, told herself that their plan now had a much greater chance of success. "Tell me," Caroline urged, "how is a gypsy wedding ceremony different from others?"

"It's very simple. The couple have been gone for about a week. Tonight they have returned and will jump over the broom together."

"And that is all it takes? Jumping over a broom?"

Elizabeth could almost see the workings of her friend's mind. "Yes," she said. "But it is only valid for gypsies."

"Too bad," Caroline said in a low voice.

The plaintive sound of violins came throbbing out of the darkness. Caroline sighed. "Oh Lizzie, listen to the music. It's so very beautiful. It makes me feel all funny inside."

"I know, dear. Me, too."

Caroline gave her a startled look. "You mean there is — someone for you?"

"Perhaps. I — I am not sure."

The tempo increased and the gypsies began to dance, whirling around the fire in mad combinations of brilliant color.

"Isn't it marvelous?" Caroline sent a look to her brother. "So very romantic."

To Elizabeth's surprise, Worthington merely nodded. The man was such a mystery to her. Imagine him agreeing that they stay the night. And why had he said that about being friends again? Could he really have meant it? Her thoughts went whirling as madly as the dancers.

The gypsy dance slowed. The violins sang a different melody, stately and sweet. Madame Nuranova appeared, a new broom in her hand. She put it carefully on the ground and backed away.

At her signal, the music changed again. It was the same melody, but underneath the sweetness, passion throbbed. Elizabeth found she was holding her breath. Caroline's grip on her arm was almost painful. Beside her, Worthington straightened.

Out of the shadows came a man and a woman. Holding hands, they walked in step. Just before they reached the broom, the music stopped. Utter silence held the meadow while the two turned and looked into each other's eyes for a long, long moment. Then, in one accord, they turned back, leaping lightly over the broom. The violins took up a gay, lilting melody and a cheer rose into the night air.

Elizabeth felt tears in her eyes and blinked rapidly. It had seemed so natural, so right. For the merest second she saw two other figures, hand in hand, leaping the broom together. Now she was getting really addlepated. Worthington had no intention of marrying. And if he ever did, it would certainly not be in the gypsy fashion. Right this moment he was probably smiling at the childish simplicity of the whole thing.

"Beautiful, isn't it?" he observed.

"What?"

"I said it's a beautiful ceremony."

"I — yes, yes, it is." She would never be able to understand him.

A smiling Madame Nuranova appeared before them. "Come," she said. "Now we dance. We feast."

A dark gypsy stopped in front of Caroline. "Dance?" he asked.

Caroline cast one look at her brother and accepted. Elizabeth, watching Worthington's face, saw the frown forming. "She's young," she said. "And this is exciting. Let her enjoy it. I promise you, it will be all right."

His frown smoothed away. "Yes. We are

just fortunate that the Lindens and their kind know nothing of this evening."

"Very fortunate," Elizabeth agreed emphatically.

He rose and offered her his arm. "I don't know about you, but I find that the day's activities have given me a vigorous appetite. Shall we see what the tables have to offer?"

"Yes," Elizabeth said. "But let's just stop there by Nanny."

The old nurse maid was firmly ensconced in the comfortable rocker. "Shall we bring you some food?" Elizabeth asked.

Nanny frowned. "I am a mite hungry. But I won't eat nothing I can't recognize."

"Yes, Nanny."

"But a nice cup of hot tea'd really taste good."

"All right, Nanny. We'll bring you some."

The tables were covered with food. Elizabeth saw Worthington eyeing some of the dishes. "Would you like to know what's in them?" she asked.

He shook his head. "Campaigning teaches a man not to ask too many questions. It's all edible, no doubt. Whatever Nanny may think."

Elizabeth laughed. "It isn't just gypsy food that Nanny dislikes. I tried to get her to taste *escargots* some time back. Our French chef made an excellent dish of them."

Worthington smiled. "And Nanny refused to eat *those disgusting snails*."

Elizabeth chuckled. "Quite."

"Were they prepared like these?" he asked, pointing to a fine china bowl.

Elizabeth picked up a flowered plate. "Let me taste one and see." She chewed for a moment. "I believe these are even better."

She watched him heap his plate with snails, with rabbit and pheasant and trout. He paused beside another bowl of meat. "I think I'm going to ask after all," he said. "Do you by chance know what meat this is?"

She nodded. *"Hotchiwichi."*

"And that is —"

"Hedgehog."

"Of course." He took several pieces, adding some bread and jam and slices from the puddings that had been boiled in cloth bags in the great iron cauldron. "A feast for a king," he said.

Elizabeth spread bread with jam, put pudding and trout on a plate, and poured a cup of tea. "I'll just take this to Nanny."

"Shall I fill your plate for you?" he asked.

She felt a wonderful warmth swelling up inside her, and a strange desire to laugh. "Yes," she said. "A little of everything."

The laughter spilled out. "But no spiders in my bread and jam, if you please."

He grinned. He looked so wonderful when he was happy. "No spiders," he repeated.

Sometime later they sat side by side, their plates empty, their stomachs full. An exhausted Caroline had given up dancing and was sitting quietly by Nanny.

The fire had burned down to embers and slowly the dancers drifted away into the darkness. And still the violins sang into the night, a plaintive, yearning melody.

Worthington got to his feet. "I ate far too much," he said. "And I feel the need for a little stroll before I retire. Would any of you ladies care to come along?"

Caroline sighed. "Not I. I have worn a hole right through my slipper, and my feet ache most dreadfully."

Nanny grunted. "These old bones want only to go to bed."

His eyes shifted to Elizabeth. "What about you?"

"Yes. I —" She wondered why she felt so strange. Her cheeks were heating up. Thank goodness the darkness prevented him from seeing her face clearly. She got up and took the arm he offered her.

"This afternoon," he said, leading her away, "I did some exploring. And I discovered a pleasant little brook." He glanced at the sky. "If the moon doesn't go behind a cloud, I can show it to you. Careful now, there may be stones."

Clinging to his arm, Elizabeth tried to quell the ridiculous pounding of her heart. She had never experienced such a feeling before. As they moved out of the clearing and into the little glade that surrounded it, the night insects made a song all their own. But overlaying it, throbbing almost in time with her heart, the violin sang on — of life and love.

The night air was cool on her heated face, and his body was warm against her side. It was most improper, of course, the two of them going off into the darkness together. Like gypsies. But Nanny had not objected.

Come to think on it, Nanny had not objected to a single thing since they had arrived at the gypsy camp. Elizabeth chuckled.

"What is amusing you?" he asked, helping her over a fallen log.

"It's Nanny. I was thinking that perhaps Madame Nuranova put a spell on her."

"She has been rather quiet," he observed.

"Perhaps it's the beauty of nature calming her."

Elizabeth laughed. "Nanny is not even fond of flowers. No, I'm afraid there's some other reason for her holding her tongue."

Worthington helped her down a grassy bank to where a little stream meandered. Stray moonbeams made little silvery glimmerings on the water.

"It's lovely," she said. "Thank you for bringing me to see it."

"You're welcome." He gestured to the bank. "Would you care to sit down for a little while?"

"Yes." Now, why should she feel suddenly breathless? And why did his eyes have such a strange look to them?

She settled in the grass, gathering the skirt of her gray traveling gown around her. It would stain, no doubt, but at the moment she didn't care.

"Look at the moon," Worthington said. "See how the wisps of cloud drift over its face."

She looked, and then she looked at him. The trees cast his face into shadow and he looked like a stranger — all but his eyes. They were the eyes of the man she knew and trusted. Then why did her heart pound so that it almost drowned out the sweet tones of the violins?

Worthington leaned toward her. "Lizzie, I —"

And suddenly the world went crazy. He pulled her against his waistcoat and his lips covered hers. Her heart seemed about to burst out of her chest and her blood went sizzling through her veins.

As abruptly as he had grabbed her, he set her from him and leapt to his feet. "Lizzie," he said. "I am abominably sorry. I have betrayed your trust. I can only say that I humbly apologize. It was the music. It went to my head. It will never happen again, I assure you. Never."

Still stunned from his kiss, she tried to make some sense of his babbling. But before she could gather her thoughts, he had pulled her to her feet and was rushing her back to the camp.

At the door to the tent, he turned to her. "Lizzie, I —"

"Goodnight," she said, as calmly as she could. "Thank you for the pleasant walk." And she lifted the flap and went in.

Actually, she was not calm at all. But Nanny and Caroline were inside that tent. She must not let them see what she was feeling.

And — even more important — she must

not let *him* see. His casual kiss must not be allowed to embarrass him. For if it did, he might sever their connection. And if he did that — She pushed the thought from her. She would not let such a thing happen.

Chapter Nine

Señorita Giaconda and her brother arrived on Monday next. Elizabeth had already put notices in the *Times* regarding the fire-eater's appearances.

Attendance at the museum had continued to swell. The caricature of the pig and Signor Cavelli had done business no harm. In fact, more than one patron had been heard to say that he had come specifically to see if he could tell "which was which."

Naturally this did not make the little Italian overly happy. He finished out his week, but only because Worthington insisted she not pay him anything till the week was done, and then he left in a spate of muttered imprecations. Actually, she had been quite pleased to see the last of him.

Signor Cavelli's temper tantrums had been hard to take. But even harder to bear had been Worthington's peculiar behavior. He had never once mentioned what had happened there beside the brook. She did not see how he expected her to pretend that it had never occurred. But that seemed to be precisely what he intended to do. He acted so strangely, was so excessively polite, that sometimes she thought she would scream.

She was dreadfully afraid that she had formed a real affection for him. But it would have to end there. For she remembered every word he had said that fateful night, every pounding of her heart when his lips touched hers. But if ever he discovered how she felt, he would most likely be gone out of her life. And she could bear almost anything rather than risk losing him.

These were the conclusions she had come to, lying there in the darkness of the gypsy tent, listening to Sarah's even breathing and Nanny's soft snores — the conclusions she had regretfully confirmed in the sleepless nights since.

On Wednesday afternoon the fire-eater was scheduled for her first appearance. A great sheet of metal carried in from the shipyard covered the stage where Signor Cavelli had performed.

Señorita Giaconda and her brother fortunately showed no temper tantrums when they discovered she was sharing billing with the learned pig. Señor Giaconda shrugged. "No matter, señorita. We come because the queen sends us. The rest is of no concern to us."

Still, as time for the first performance approached, Elizabeth felt the onset of nerves. The museum had turned out to be much more trouble than she had ever envisioned. It was worth it, of course, to make her father's dream come true, but sometimes she wished she could be shut of the whole thing.

She did not intend to let Worthington know this, however. He would only insist that he had been right all along. She paused. Perhaps he had been. But she wasn't ready to concede that. Not yet, at least.

Worthington arrived about half an hour before the scheduled performance time. He smiled as he crossed the floor toward her, making her heart skip about in such an erratic fashion she feared he would hear its crazy thumping.

"Good day, Lizzie," he said. "All ready?"

"Yes."

"Has Toby — or rather, Mr. Ware — been keeping up to snuff?"

She nodded. "I had a good talk with that man, you know. I told him such drunken behavior could not be tolerated."

He smiled. "No doubt he agreed."

"Of course." His expression gave her the feeling she was missing something, but she

146

didn't continue the discussion. Probably it was just her nerves. She hadn't been sleeping at all well. "Did Caroline come with you?"

He looked around. "Yes. She's about somewhere. Said she was looking for something."

It was not some*thing,* but some*one,* that Caroline was looking for — Señor Giaconda. But this was not the time to inform Worthington about that. Let him notice little things himself. Let him begin to suspect something.

Elizabeth tried to calm her ragged nerves. This was dangerous business they had embarked on — this endeavor to persuade Worthington that James Mitchell was an appropriate husband for his sister. She did not see how she could back down now, though, not when Caroline was depending on her. But if Worthington ever discovered that she had conspired with his sister . . .

"Lizzie!" From the tone of his voice he had already spoken to her more than once.

"Yes, yes. What is it?"

"For heaven's sake, don't look so startled. Anyone would think you were frightened to death." He frowned. "Has something gone wrong that I don't know about?"

"No, no." She hastened to reassure him.

She'd better be more careful, or she'd be giving the thing away herself. "Everything is fine. I just talked to Mr. Ware. He's through for the day. And her brother says Señorita Giaconda is ready to perform."

Worthington sighed. "And here come the Lindens. Right on schedule."

Elizabeth fixed a smile on her face, but she was afraid it looked as false as it felt. Still, the Lindens were a recurring plague. Every new attraction brought them out, and she no longer had any doubt that every time they were hoping she would meet with disaster.

"Dear Lady Elizabeth," Miss Linden gushed. "How clever of you to engage such an attraction." She lowered her voice. "I hear that the fire-eater is a *woman*. And she travels with her brother — or at least he *says* he's her brother."

Elizabeth could hardly believe her ears. The simplest fact turned sinister the moment it left Miss Linden's tongue. "Yes," Elizabeth said, keeping her voice pleasant. "Her brother kindly consented to accompany her here."

Plainly, neither of the Lindens was willing to accept this truth. Elizabeth swallowed a sigh. How could one deal with such people?

The chimes rang, announcing the performance, and the Lindens scurried away. Worthington, looking after them, shook his head and offered Lizzie his arm. "*Those* two should be on exhibit," he remarked. "Surely there are no others like them anywhere."

"I should hope not," Lizzie exclaimed.

Worthington glanced down at her. He was not at all happy about the way she looked. This paleness of hers was most unusual. Running the museum was a strain on her, but he could see no way to get her to give it up.

Perhaps the kiss had upset her. He couldn't believe he'd done such a thing — and when she trusted him, too. She'd been rather quiet and exceedingly polite the last several days. If he had angered her and she refused to honor their agreement, how could he look out for her? And now, more than ever, he was convinced that she needed him.

He maneuvered them into a place where Lizzie could see Lady Linden's extravagant bonnet bobbing in the front row. He was sure that minutes after the performance ended, word of its every detail would have spread through the entire city.

The gypsy stood beside his sister on the improvised stage. "Señors y señoritas," he said. "Señorita Giaconda will now perform."

The crowd hushed, gazing at her in expectation.

"First, she passes lighted candles under her bare arms." A murmur went through the crowd as the señorita did just that.

"Now she drops sealing wax upon her tongue." The murmur grew louder as the hot wax fell.

"Now she cooks for you an egg. Into her hands I pour the boiling oil." A collective gasp issued from the crowd, all their concentration focused on the oil. "Now I drop in the egg."

There was a pause of about a minute. Worthington surveyed the crowd. Clearly, the señorita was impressing it. And then, from somewhere near the front, came an all-too-familiar voice. "I don't believe it. It's a trick."

Beside him Lizzie muttered some words unfit for female tongues. "Why?" she whispered. "Why does she do this?"

"Don't worry," he consoled her. "I'm sure the gypsy can handle her."

And he was right. The Spaniard quickly singled out Miss Linden. "If the señorita will come up here, I will give to her the egg — to eat."

Miss Linden ascended the stage, accepting the egg in her outstretched hand. "It's already been cooked," she declared, "before you came out here. I wager that oil isn't even hot."

Señor Giaconda nodded gravely. "Then the señorita will be glad to put a finger in it."

Miss Linden drew back a step. "Oh, I couldn't do that!"

The crowd, cheated of the anticipated spectacle, began to turn ugly. "Then get out the way!"

"Shut yer mouth and let the fire-eater get on with it!"

"Yeah. Get out. We come to see the fire proof woman, not no la-dee."

Miss Linden descended the stage in a flurry of skirts. Lizzie, her spirits much refreshed, chuckled. "That girl will never learn."

"There you are, Lizzie," Caroline said, rushing up. "Isn't the señorita marvelous? And her brother is quite dashing. I was talking to him a while ago. He's really a remarkable fellow."

"Remarkable?" He felt the pressure of Lizzie's fingers on his arm and knew it for a subtle warning, but Caroline was so young, so foolish. And he was responsible for the girl.

"Yes," she continued. "They have traveled through Spain and France and Germany. And did you know, he plays the violin?"

He didn't like the look on her face — that dewy-eyed look. But the chit was young, and perhaps Lizzie knew something he didn't. "No," he contented himself with saying. "I didn't know that."

"Well, he does." Caroline turned a glowing face to Lizzie. "I just love gypsy music. It's so — so —"

"It is beautiful," Lizzie said. "But so is other music. Mr. Haydn's. Or —"

"I could listen to gypsy violins forever," Caroline breathed.

He could feel his temper rising. The chit had to learn some sense. "Caroline —" he began.

And then pandemonium broke loose. Someone started shouting. "The pig! Oh God! The pig's gone mad! He's foaming at the mouth!"

The crowd shattered, people rushing about, some this way, some that, before the pandemonium became a mad scramble for the door. Shoving Lizzie and his sister to safety behind a display, Worthington stepped out, intent on reasoning with the crowd. But before he could open his mouth, a burly farmer shouldered him aside, sending him sprawling against the wall, where his head hit the paneling with a sharp *thwack*. By the time the room quit whirling, everyone was gone.

He started to push himself erect.

"Tom-Tom, are you hurt?"

Lizzie's fingers were cool against his brow. He was tempted to claim an injury and let her care for him. But if the pig were truly mad, something must be done.

"I'm all right," he insisted, getting to his feet. "You two stay here. I've got to find the pig."

"But I —"

He grabbed her by the shoulders. "Lizzie! Listen to me! You and Caroline stay out of the way. If the pig is truly mad, he could be dangerous."

"Then you should —"

"Stay here," he yelled.

He left her there, gaping after him, and hurried into the next room. The pig was there, all right, all 600 pounds of him, and there was foam around his mouth. But from the peculiar way he listed to one side, it did not appear that he was actually mad.

"Mr. Ware!"

"Yes, milord?" The ruddy Mr. Ware peeked out from behind a display case.

"Come here."

153

The showman shuffled out, listing almost as much as the pig. "Whatcha want?"

The lout needed a lesson in manners, but that would have to wait. "What is wrong with your pig?"

Mr. Ware shook his head sagely. "Ain't nothing wrong with him. Toby, he's happier 'an a lark."

"Then why is he foaming at the mouth?"

The pig took a step and collapsed with a loud groan. Mr. Ware hiccuped. "He's in his cups, he is." Mr. Ware chuckled drunkenly. "Or actually, in his pail."

"You mean —"

"Aye. We shared my pail of gin. He's got a real fondness for gin, ya see. And then, later, when I was washing my shirt — well, I ain't got but one pail. And Toby, he thought it was more gin. And he dipped his snout in the suds. And fore I could get him cleaned up, some'un sees him and starts in screaming. Then they all goes wild."

Mr. Ware sighed. "We didn't mean to make no trouble — Toby and me. We was done for the day and we was just having us a drop — to relax."

Worthington was hard put not to laugh, though it was difficult *not* to laugh at 600 pounds of drunken pig. "Better get Toby back to your room. Can you do that?"

Mr. Ware slowly nodded. "I'm thinking so, milord. Course, I could do it real quick if I had me a pail of gin."

Worthington swallowed a frown. Mr. Ware was nothing if not persevering. "I'm afraid that's impossible. I've no one to send. But if you get Toby back to his room, then you can go get some gin for both of you. And I'll stand the bill."

Mr. Ware rubbed his red nose and looked relieved. "You'll tell the lady that we can have it? She don't seem to understand what a man needs."

"I'll see that she understands. Just get Toby back to the room."

With much coaxing and prodding, Mr. Ware got Toby to his feet once more. "You come along, now, like a good pig. We'll just go back to our beds an' I'll go get us some gin."

At the word "gin," the pig squealed and began to move faster.

Confident that Toby would soon be out of sight, Worthington turned back the way he'd come. "Lizzie! Caroline!"

The two women were waiting where he had left them. Lizzie was quite pale, but Caroline was conducting an animated conversation with that gypsy fellow. She turned as he came up.

"Oh, Worthington, Señor Giaconda came back to see if we were all right. Wasn't that kind of him?"

"Very." He didn't like the color in his sister's cheeks or the gleam in her eye, but he would remonstrate with her later.

Right then he was worried about Lizzie. She looked almost ill. "It's all right," he said, hurrying to her side. "The pig is not mad. He dipped his snout in Mr. Ware's washpail and —"

Caroline began to laugh, but Lizzie made a strange little sound — half moan, half gurgle — and sank toward the floor. He caught her just in time, breaking her fall.

"Lizzie!" Caroline cried. "Oh dear, whatever is wrong with her?"

The Spaniard shrugged. "The señorita was *muy* frightened." He looked at Worthington. "She was much worried about the señor."

Standing there, holding her limp body in his arms, he could hardly believe it. Surely Lizzie could not have swooned away out of fear for him. Not Lizzie! "But I have not even been injured."

"The señor will excuse, but there is blood on his cheek."

Caroline's eyes widened. "You must have scratched yourself when you fell."

"It's nothing. I didn't even know it was there." Lizzie was not getting any lighter. "Where can I put her?"

Caroline spread her cloak on the floor. "Put her here," she said. "The poor thing is so dreadfully pale."

He put her gently down and knelt to chafe her wrists. "Lizzie, come on now. Wake up."

Her eyes opened slowly, then widened at the sight of him. "I'm all right," he said quickly. "It's just a scratch."

She gave him a weak smile and tried to sit up.

"No," he said. "Not yet. Now, when did you eat last?"

"I — I don't remember. Breakfast, I guess, but tell me. Why did Toby have his head in Mr. Ware's pail?"

He frowned. "The pig thought it held gin."

Caroline burst into laughter. "The pig *does* imbibe. I wonder —"

"Caroline, be sensible. Lizzie is ill."

She pushed herself into a sitting position. "No, no. I am fine. But Worthington, what shall I do? We cannot have a drunken pig running loose through the place. People will not come."

Again she had asked for his advice. "I

don't think Toby will give us any more trouble," he said. "Mr. Ware enticed him back to his room."

She frowned. "Enticed?"

He nodded. "I told him he could go get some more gin if he got Toby out of sight. I told him it would be all right with you."

He waited for the explosion. But it didn't come. "Of course," she said.

Of course! That settled it. When Lizzie let him take charge, when she said "of course" in that weird tone of voice — something must be very wrong.

He turned to the Spaniard. "Call the carriage, please, Señor Giaconda. And you and your sister may have the rest of the day off. Caroline, go get Mr. Elderby. Tell him to put up the Closed sign. We're taking Lizzie home."

Chapter Ten

For two days Worthington refused to let Elizabeth return to the museum. He insisted that it would run quite well without her — and indeed, it did. Mr. Elderby managed everything to perfection.

She languished about the house, feeling sometimes ridiculous and sometimes angry. If this was love, the poets had been sadly misinformed about its glory. Quite often she told herself that she wished that kiss had never happened.

But such feelings didn't last long. Then she fell to remembering each detail of that magic night, wondering what it would be like to be Worthington's wife.

She longed to confide in someone. But Caroline was too open to long keep such a secret. It was rather surprising that she had succeeded in hiding her love for James Mitchell as long as she had.

And, though Sarah was the soul of discretion, Elizabeth did not want to impinge on her happiness. Sarah was radiant in the belief that Vidon soon meant to ask for her.

And Elizabeth herself felt certain this was the case. Half the gypsy's prediction had come true, at least.

So Elizabeth kept her peace, alternating between joy and despair, trying to cultivate a philosophical attitude and quite failing at it.

She shuddered still when she remembered seeing that blood on Worthington's face. But she could not quite grasp the fact that she had swooned. Never in her life had she felt the least faint — until that moment when he had appeared with blood on his cheek.

She told herself it was a perfectly natural reaction. She had not been sleeping or eating well. Food had lost its savor and most of her nights were spent in reliving every word, every gesture, of that precious time by the brook.

She did not blame him for the kiss. It was quite understandable. And certainly she had acquiesced in the act. She only wished their kiss could have been caused by a better reason than his blood being heated by gypsy music. But he had made it clear that he had no romantic interest in her, that it had all been a mistake. She struggled to accept that.

And so she passed her time until the afternoon of the third day. She'd been trying to rest, but the feeling of being shut up was beginning to prey on her nerves. If only Worthington would come to call.

Almost as though in answer to her wish, Barton appeared in the doorway. "A caller, milady."

Her heart rose up in her throat. At last he had come. "Who is it?"

"The Viscount Vidon."

"He's alone?"

"Yes, milady."

Her heart fell. "Call Miss Calvert, then."

"If you please, milady, the viscount wishes to speak to you alone."

"Of course. Send him in."

Vidon was patently nervous. He perched on the edge of a chair and kept pulling at his cravat as though it choked him.

"Good afternoon," she said. "I understand you wish to speak to me."

"Yes. I —" He yanked at his coat sleeve like a schoolboy. "Dash it, Lady Elizabeth, I've never done this thing before."

She swallowed a smile. "I'm afraid I don't know what *thing* you're doing."

"Why, I'm trying to — that is — well, I want to marry Sarah!"

"I see."

"And you being her only relative, so to

speak, well, I thought I should apply to you."

"You're quite right. So, how does Sarah feel about this?"

"She — she has said she will accept me . . . but only if we have your blessing."

How like Sarah. "Of course you have it."

His smile was a joy to see. "Oh, thank you."

"There's just one thing."

"Yes?"

"Your friend Worthington is not going to be pleased by this. You know he meant you for his sister."

Vidon's smile faded. "I know. But we don't suit. Not a bit. Why can't he see that?"

She shrugged. "We are all blind about some things. When do you plan to tell him?"

His look turned sheepish. "I was hoping — that is, I thought that you — you have so much influence on him."

She stared. "I? You're quite mistaken."

He smiled weakly. "I think not."

"Well, still, I cannot interfere with his decisions. But I have already told him you were wrong for his sister."

"And what did he say?"

"He told me that that wasn't important."

The viscount shook his head. "If he were once in love, really in love, he would know better. I cannot imagine being married to anyone but Sarah."

"And the marquis cannot imagine being married at all."

Vidon chuckled. "He will. One of these days he will meet his match. He'll be leg-shackled, no doubt of it."

Her heart began to pound and her knees to quiver. It was difficult enough the way it was. But if he married, if some other woman . . . she pressed a hand to her forehead.

"Lady Elizabeth, are you ill?"

"No, no. I'm fine. Please, ring and tell Barton to find Sarah for you."

"I think she's waiting in the garden."

"Then go to her and tell her you have my blessing."

Vidon bounded to his feet. "Thank you, you're a real lady."

He was gone before she could reply and she was left to consider the changes she would soon have to make in her household. It would be different without Sarah, lonely. She could look for another companion, of course. But it would be hard to find someone with a character as sweet as Sarah's.

Then Sarah came running in and threw her arms about her. "Dear Elizabeth! I am so very happy. Thank you."

Elizabeth smiled. "You've nothing to thank me for, dear. You deserve happiness."

"And so do you," Sarah said, sobering. "But remember, what Madame Nuranova said came true for me. It will come true for you, too. I know it."

Though Elizabeth nodded, Sarah's words gave her little comfort. Worthington had said very clearly that he did not mean to marry. When they were children, she had sometimes pestered him till he did what she wanted. But one could hardly badger a man into matrimony!

Barton appeared in the doorway. "The Marquis of Worthington, milady."

Why did he have to come now, when Vidon was there with this disconcerting news? She struggled to compose herself. It was not her fault the viscount had chosen Sarah. Surely Worthington could see that.

"Lizzie, I —" He stopped and looked at his friend.

Vidon turned pale, but he faced the marquis manfully. "Afternoon, Worthington. You're just in time."

"Time for what?"

"To help us rejoice," said Sarah with a warm smile. "The viscount has asked me to marry him. And Elizabeth has said that I may."

Elizabeth saw Worthington's face darken, but then his features smoothed out again. "My congratulations," he said, extending his hand to his friend.

Elizabeth breathed a sigh of relief. Sarah's joy shouldn't be dampened by any disturbance between the men.

Worthington continued to smile. "Would you mind leaving us alone?" he said. "I have a matter to discuss with Elizabeth."

Vidon looked only too pleased to escape. "Of course. Sarah and I have much to decide on."

They were barely out the door when Worthington turned to Elizabeth with an accusing look. "You saw this coming."

"Yes. I told you it would happen."

He settled into a chair. "I suppose it cannot be helped. Once a man falls in love, he gets besotted. Still, I am worried about Caroline. Vidon would have been just right for her."

"To your mind, not to Caroline's."

He sighed heavily. "Yes . . . I suppose you're right. But what shall I do?"

"Do?" He was asking *her?*

"The chit needs a husband."

"Have you one in mind?"

He shook his head. "No. I've been over it and over it. Trying to think of someone."

"I suppose they were all lords."

He looked startled. "Of course. She can't marry a commoner."

"You know my feelings on that."

He frowned. "Quite well. Just don't mention them to Caroline."

"Do you think *she* has someone in mind to marry?"

He avoided her eyes. She was just as glad, though, since she'd never been good at lying.

"I'm almost afraid to say it. But I think she's taken to this gypsy fellow."

"Señor Giaconda? Surely you're wrong." She hoped she'd put just the right tone of amazement in her voice.

He sighed again. "I wish I were. But she's always going about humming those gypsy melodies. And enthusing on the traveling life." He threw up his hands. "Why can't the chit fall in love with an Englishman?"

"I don't know." Poor Tom-Tom. For a moment she wanted to tell him the truth. But Caroline was depending on her. "Have you anyone in mind?"

"I told you, I've run over the whole list of eligibles. I wouldn't trust my sister to any of them."

She took a deep breath. Here was the opening she'd been waiting for. "Then perhaps you should look elsewhere."

He glared at her. "Look where?"

"You've just said there are no suitable lords. It follows, therefore, that you'll have to think of commoners."

"Lizzie —"

"Let's see — you want a sober man, hardworking, kind, generous, well-educated, able to make a living. Have you anything to add?"

He stared at her. "I think you've taken leave of your senses. If I could find such a paragon — which seems highly unlikely — how could I persuade him to ask for Caroline? Or her to have him?"

She swallowed hastily. This was dangerous ground. "If I think the fellow is suitable, I will help you persuade her. I think I have some influence over her."

"I know you do." He gave her a rueful smile. "I tell you, if you help me in this you'll have my undying gratitude."

It was not gratitude she wanted from him, but she, too, managed a smile. "Remember, he should be young and relatively nice-looking."

"Yes, yes. I'll remember. I know she's young and romantic. But who —"

"You will think of someone." If only it was the *right* someone. And if James Mitchell didn't refuse . . .

She decided to change the subject. "Worthington, I must go back to the museum tomorrow. I assure you, I am perfectly well."

He frowned thoughtfully. "You do look better. And you're eating?"

"Yes. And I must be there if I'm to look out for Caroline, to persuade her that gypsies do not make good husbands."

He nodded. "I'll pick you up tomorrow, then. In the meantime, think on this husband thing. I've got to get that girl married right. I promised my father." Absently, he rubbed his shoulder. "And you know how I am about such promises."

"Yes. I know."

He got to his feet and looked around. "Where is that creature that masquerades as a dog?"

"He's in disgrace. For demolishing my slipper."

Worthington chuckled. "No doubt he took it because he had no ankles to chew on. I'll see you tomorrow."

From behind the curtains she watched him get into his barouche. She stood at the window looking long after he'd driven out

168

of sight. If Caroline played her part as she should, if the gypsy kept his end of the bargain, if James Mitchell really did care about the girl . . . with all those ifs, they had only a small chance of success. And not even that, unless Worthington could be led to settle on James Mitchell.

She must prepare a list of men. James Mitchell's name would be on it. And all the others would be selected because there was something about them that Worthington couldn't abide. And so eventually, there would be only Mitchell left. Pray God they could make this work.

If they could, Caroline and Sarah would both be brides. While she — she swallowed an oath. She had hoped and prayed for Sarah to win Vidon. She was helping Caroline to a wedding with the man she loved. But when it came to Worthington, she could not come up with a single idea on how to gain his affection for herself.

She sighed. If only they were gypsies! If only they were there by the brook again, with the moon shining down and the violins throbbing. She straightened, laughter rising to her lips. That was it! That was the answer!

Hurrying to her writing desk, she began a note to Madame Nuranova.

★ ★ ★

As he headed homeward, Worthington's mind was a mass of racing thoughts. Perhaps Lizzie was right. A younger son might be all right. Someone Caroline could really care about. Anyone but that gypsy fellow — and a Spaniard, yet!

Played the violin, did he? Curse those violins. It was their music that had led him into temptation, made him kiss Lizzie like she was some common — he couldn't bring himself to finish the thought. And the worst of it was, he wanted to kiss her again. If he hadn't been convinced, it would mean the end of their friendship, he might even have asked her to marry him. And what a laugh she would get from that!

Oh, it was patently clear. Lizzie wanted him for a friend. She didn't want him for a husband. Probably, she, too, wanted some romantic chap who would make her heart sing.

He glanced at his timepiece. The Little Dove would be waiting. He frowned and directed the coachman to turn toward home instead. The Little Dove was fast losing her appeal. Her conversation was insipid, and her charms . . . Why, he'd rather be with Lizzie, discussing Toby's drunkenness and Mr. Ware's dereliction from duty.

He sighed. If only he could ask Lizzie to marry him without jeopardizing their friendship. It was something he would have to think on. But first he had to get Caroline safely wed, before the chit decided to run off with that gypsy!

The next few days passed quickly. Elizabeth returned to the museum. The scare over the pig had not affected attendance as she'd feared, and for a change, everything was running smoothly. It was a good thing, too, because she could not concentrate on the museum and its problems.

It was all fine and good to tell herself she would treat Worthington as she always had. But when he was with her, she was torn between the terrifying urge to cast herself into his arms and the equally ridiculous desire to sit in the corner and cry.

She waited impatiently for an answer to her message to the gypsy queen. When it finally came, Madame Nuranova said she had found several possibilities, among them a horned lady and a man who escaped from various confinements.

Elizabeth didn't really care what the prospects did, she wanted desperately to get back to the gypsy camp, to get Worthington there. And so when he arrived on Tuesday afternoon, she was again feeling somewhat nervous.

Caroline was with him, her broad smile attesting to the fact that so far, things were running smoothly. "I'll just look around," she said.

Worthington frowned and Elizabeth hastened to say, "Wait just a moment. I have heard from Madame Nuranova. She has some more possibilities for the museum. She — she invites us to come see them next week."

The most peculiar expression crossed Worthington's face. If only she could decipher it.

"Do you think you are up to another journey?" he asked.

"I'm fine. I told you — I was just working too hard. A little trip will be good for me."

"I can look after the museum," Caroline volunteered.

"Indeed, you won't." Worthington's scowl was instantaneous. Then he apparently had second thoughts. "That is, I think you'd better come along. Lizzie may need you."

Elizabeth was about to say that she needed no one, but she kept her tongue between her teeth. It was obvious that he didn't mean to leave his sister alone in the city.

Caroline pouted, probably for real, since she would be denied the chance to see James Mitchell.

"Come now," Elizabeth said. "Your brother knows best."

The two of them stared at her. "Well, what is so strange about my saying that?" she demanded. "Worthington is a man of the world. He has experience and knowledge. We should listen to him."

His eyes twinkled. "You, Lizzie? Listen to *me?*"

She smiled. "You needn't make such a fuss. Now, when can we go?"

He considered for a moment. "How about Monday? You can keep the Giacondas on for another week. Then, if we find someone appropriate, you can hire a new attraction."

Caroline looked suitably unhappy, as well she might. If the Spaniards left too soon, their plot might fail.

"Yes," Elizabeth answered. "Or we might let Toby go. I'm not at all sure about that pig."

Worthington laughed. "The pig can't buy the gin, you know. If I were going to worry, I should worry about Mr. Ware. But don't. I think they will behave themselves."

Chapter Eleven

The first of the next week found them arriving at the gypsy camp. Because of Caroline's coming along, Sarah had been excused. That meant Worthington had shared the carriage with his sister, Lizzie, and Nanny Coulter.

As he helped the women descend, he looked around. This camp was set up in the usual fashion, all the tents and benders facing south, the woods at their back.

Worthington swallowed a sigh. Seeing the gypsy camp again made the memory of that kiss even more vivid. And he didn't need to be reminded of it, not at all.

He was hard put to know how to behave around Lizzie these days. Every time he saw her, he was plagued by the most dreadful desire to crush her to his waistcoat and kiss her madly. Such thoughts had occupied his mind for several hours of the journey and had not put him into a particularly affable mood. He admitted to himself that it was quite probably only the presence of his sister and the old nurse that had kept him from succumbing to temptation and turning his thoughts into reality.

The gypsy queen appeared to welcome them, smiling broadly. "My telling for the fair one has come true. Soon she weds."

Lizzie looked startled. "How did you know that?"

Madame Nuranova smiled mysteriously. "Gypsies have ways. Come, you see what I tell you about."

Worthington offered Lizzie his arm and the other two trailed after. He smiled to see that Madame Nuranova had the rocking chair ready. Nanny sank into it with a sigh of relief. "You're the kindest creature," she told the gypsy queen. "I thank you."

Madame Nuranova smiled. "Hot tea comes." She turned to the others. "Seats for you, too. The people are ready."

Worthington assisted Lizzie to a seat and took one beside her.

"First," said the gypsy queen, "is horned woman." She clapped her hands and a woman emerged from behind one of the tents. She wore drab brown and her head was completely covered by a black veil.

She came to a stop before them and at a signal from the gypsy, raised the veil. The face under it was far from attractive. And in the middle of the forehead grew a protuberance that looked more like a big bump than a horn.

After a few moments, Lizzie said gently, "Thank you. That is enough."

The woman replaced the veil and glided off to one side to wait.

The gypsy queen clapped again. Two burly fellows appeared, carrying a trunk. "Monsieur Rience," Madame Nuranova said. "He gets in the trunk. All is locked. Chains put around. Within two minutes he is out."

Worthington straightened in his chair. Confinement in such a space was more than he could imagine. And he knew with certainty that *he* would not willingly undertake such a thing.

Lizzie drew in a breath. "How can he do it?"

"I don't know. There must be some trick to it."

The Frenchman appeared. A dapper little man, he hardly seemed strong enough to stand under the weight of the chains they loaded him with.

When his helpers had him suitably chained, they looked to Worthington. "Please, milord — you will examine the locks?"

He got to his feet. "I'll just take a look."

The locks all seemed strong. When he had said so, the little man nodded gravely. "*Merci,* milord."

With the aid of his cohorts, Monsieur Rience stepped into the trunk and settled down. The lid shut with a threatening *thud* and exterior chains were bound around it and locked. Worthington winced. He distinctly heard the click of the locking tumblers.

The assistants pulled a gaily colored screen in front of the trunk, took out their timepieces, and began to count off the seconds in unison. At one minute and forty-nine seconds, a smiling Monsieur Rience emerged from behind the screen.

"Well, now," said Nanny. "If that ain't something else."

Lizzie nodded. "Indeed, it's very interesting." She turned to Worthington. "I don't think we can hire the woman, do you?"

He shook his head. "No."

"The poor thing." Lizzie reached in her reticule and gave him a guinea. "Please, explain to her and give her this. I'll speak to Monsieur Rience."

"All right, but don't offer him too much."

She smiled. "Only what I've been paying the others."

★ ★ ★

He found the woman by one of the
benders. "We cannot hire you for the
museum," he said, keeping his tone gentle.
"We are more interested in performances
like the man's."

"I understand."

"But the lady would like you to have this
for your trouble."

She looked down at the coin. "Thank 'ee.
Milord?"

"Yes?"

"Could you be giving me some smaller
coins in trade?"

"Why?"

The veiled head bowed. "Me man, he'll
be that angry. So I'll have to give him somewhat. If I give him this, won't be nothing for
the young ones."

"I understand." He took out some coins,
more than a guinea's worth. "Take these
then. And keep the guinea, too."

She gave him a brilliant smile. "God's
blessings be on you and your lady," she said.

"She's not —" he began, but she was has-
tening away.

He turned — and found the gypsy queen
behind him.

"You do not have wife yet?" she asked.

"No."

"But you know woman you want."

How could she have guessed? "No. I —"

"You still invite me to wedding?"

"If you could bring it off, I'd be glad to." Whatever was he doing, talking to this gypsy as though she could really help him?

"I know what you need. You need love powder."

Oh, now, he was really in the suds. She meant to sell him something, no doubt for an outrageous price.

"I give you powder," she said, her glance furtive. "But you don't let Elizabeth know."

"Really, I —"

She reached into the pocket of her skirt. "This makes woman want man."

"But —"

She pressed it into his hand — a little packet of powder. "You put pinch in drink. She want you."

"Madame Nuranova, really —"

She shrugged. "I know. You have no belief. So? Belief is not needed. Powder works without belief." She smiled. "What harm is in trying?"

"None, I suppose." He was feeling really ridiculous and in an effort to regain his lost dignity, he said, "I — ah — there is something you could do for me."

"Ask. For Elizabeth's friend we do anything."

"I — well, Elizabeth has a collection of shrunken heads. I should like to add to it. So, if in your travels you would watch for some — in good condition, of course. Maybe you could purchase them for me. And keep it a secret from Liz— Elizabeth. I should like to surprise her."

The gypsy nodded. "This I will do. You are good man." She gave him a quizzical smile. "You are not so angry now."

To his surprise he realized that she was right. "No. I'm not." He reached in his pocket. "May I give you something —"

She frowned. "I give powder as gift. Elizabeth is gypsies' friend. We owe her much."

It suddenly occurred to him that he would be wanting Caroline to fall in love with the man of his choice. "How — how does the powder work?"

"You put in tea. The first man she sees after she drinks — him she will want."

"I — ah, I see. Well, I'd better get back to Elizabeth."

"Remember, she is not to know this."

"Yes, yes, I'll remember." As if he would ever tell Lizzie that he meant to use a love powder to make her his wife!

★ ★ ★

Elizabeth, having concluded her business with Monsieur Rience, gave herself up to remembering the little brook and the moonlight, the feel of Worthington's arms around her, the touch of his lips . . .

"Is your business all concluded?" he asked.

His sudden appearance, combined with her thoughts, made her cheeks go hot. "Yes, yes. I believe so." She looked with longing toward the woods, but she found herself unable to utter a word about walking there.

"Then I suppose we should start for home."

"Yes, I suppose so. Just let me have a word with Madame Nuranova."

"Of course. I'll take the others to the carriage."

She watched as he led Nanny and Caroline away. Then Elizabeth turned to the gypsy queen. "Thank you for your help. I truly appreciate it."

The gypsy nodded. "You need other help? Your man — he does not ask?"

"I — how did you know?"

"I see in your eyes when you look at him. I know love."

Elizabeth sighed. "He doesn't love me. And, and I don't know how to change that."

Madame Nuranova sent a furtive glance toward the others, who were now out of earshot. "I fix that." She reached in the pocket of her brightly colored skirt and extended a small packet to Elizabeth. "Put away quick. Tell no one."

Elizabeth hid the packet in her reticule. "What is it?"

"Love powder," the gypsy said. "Put pinch in tea. You serve him. He will want you."

The blood that had rushed to Elizabeth's cheeks drained swiftly away. "You mean —"

"He will ask." The gypsy glanced over her shoulder. "He comes. Do not tell."

Elizabeth tried to act natural as Worthington led her to the carriage. But this was the outside of enough. Here she was — a sane, sensible woman who had always prided herself on her intelligence, believing in gypsy predictions and love powders. But oh, if only the powder would work!

By Friday midday Elizabeth had completed her list of possible husbands for Caroline. To Worthington, each name would seem logical. And only she knew that she had chosen each with infinite care, to assure that James Mitchell would be the only really suitable one.

When Worthington arrived to take her home for lunch, he came alone. The carriage had hardly started to move before he said, "How are you coming with the list?"

"I have all the names I can think of. Would you care to join me for lunch?"

"I'm not hungry. Just let me come in and get the names."

Soon they were in her library. "Now," he said impatiently, "give me the names."

One by one she read them off. And one by one he shook his head. Finally she came to the last name. "James Mitchell."

Worthington shot her a startled look. "My steward?"

Elizabeth nodded.

"Whatever made you settle on him?"

She shrugged. "He seemed to have all the right qualities. And you have always spoken highly of him."

He frowned. "As a steward, not as a brother-in-law."

"You have had ample opportunity to observe him."

"True."

"And you have found no fault with him."

"True."

She set her tongue between her teeth then and willed herself to stay silent. If he did not settle on James Mitchell now, there was nothing more she could do. Pressing Worthington would only make him suspicious.

Finally he nodded. "I suppose it might work. Let's see, how shall I go about it?"

She swallowed her sigh of relief. "First I would ask Mitchell. There is no point in saying anything to Caroline until he has agreed."

"That's right. For all we know, the man may have an affection for someone else."

She prayed that was not the case. Caroline must be right about Mitchell's feelings for her, else the whole plan was doomed. "When shall you approach him?"

Worthington frowned. "As soon as I can. May I send Caroline over here, on some sort of errand?"

"Of course."

Arriving home a short time later, Worthington summoned his sister. "Please go to Elizabeth's and ask her when Monsieur Rience is expected to arrive."

Caroline got eagerly to her feet. "Is she at the museum?"

He managed to contain his frown. "No, she's at home."

Caroline sighed. "I wanted to go to the museum."

"Whatever for? You've been there every day since the place opened."

"I know. But it is — interesting. You — you want me to learn things, don't you?"

"Yes." Indeed he did. But not from a gypsy! "But I would like you to come straight home today."

"What for?"

"I — ah — want to know what Lizzie says."

When Caroline sighed, he frowned. This looked serious. Just so did he sigh when he thought of Lizzie.

"Very well," she said. "I'll be back soon."

She'd been gone for several minutes, ample time to be out of the house, but Worthington still did not move, except to pull nervously at his cravat. This infernal heat — he sighed. It was not the heat that was making him uncomfortable, but the task that lay before him, a task he was loath to undertake. Well, he would learn nothing sitting there. And he had never been a coward.

He made his way to the study where Mitchell, bent over the desk, was adding up lists of figures.

"Good afternoon, milord," the steward said.

"Afternoon, Mitchell." Worthington

stopped. He was feeling more and more the fool.

Mitchell looked up. "Did you wish something, milord?"

"Yes, I — that is — dash it, man, this is most uncomfortable."

Mitchell frowned and got to his feet. "Have I done something to displease you, milord?"

"Good grief, no! You're the best steward a man could ask for!"

"Then what is it?"

"It's — it's another sort of position I want you to fill."

Mitchell looked puzzled, as well he might. "I'm afraid I don't understand."

"It's that sister of mine. She needs a husband."

Mitchell was silent, but his face registered shock.

"You — I — that is — dash it, man. I want you to marry my sister."

He had never seen a man turn pasty-white so quickly. Mitchell sat down with a thud. "Me, milord?"

"Yes."

"But —"

"You're decent, honest, upright —"

"But I've no title. And no expectation of one."

"I know that. It doesn't signify." Lord, he was sounding more like Lizzie every day.

"Doesn't signify?" repeated Mitchell, obviously dazed.

"That's right. You see, the silly chit's got her eye on this gypsy fellow, the fire-eater's brother."

"The gypsy?"

"Right. Now, I want my sister safely married. And I've chosen you."

For several minutes the room was silent. Mitchell was still exceedingly pale. He seemed stunned.

Finally Worthington spoke. "I suppose this means, that you won't do it."

"No, no, milord!" Mitchell frowned. "I am trying to think how to tell you this. I have had an affection for your sister for some time. I did not speak of it to her, of course. I knew you wished her to marry the Viscount Vidon."

Worthington nodded. "So I did. But the viscount had other ideas. He plans to marry someone else."

"I — do you suppose your sister will have me?"

Worthington sighed. "I do not know. But I cannot have her running off with this gypsy fellow." He reached into his pocket. "Listen, I know it sounds silly. Really ridiculous. But the gypsy queen gave me some powder. Just a pinch in Caroline's tea and she will want you."

If the matter hadn't been so serious, he'd have laughed at the peculiar expression crossing Mitchell's face. "I know, I know. But in a case like this, we must use any means available." And if the stuff worked on Caroline, he would try it on Lizzie. Damned if he wouldn't!

Mitchell stared down at the packet in his hand. "A pinch in her tea? And she will love me?"

"So the gypsy said. Listen, Caroline will be back soon. Do the best you can. She likes that romantic stuff, you know. And Liz— Lady Elizabeth has promised to help persuade her to take you. You know Caroline listens to her."

"A pinch in her tea," Mitchell repeated in disbelief.

Worthington clapped him on the shoulder. "Come on, man. Buck up. She's only a woman."

Mitchell flushed. "I'm sorry, milord. But I have worshipped her from afar for so long, not daring even to hope. And now — to have this happen . . . It is difficult to comprehend."

"I know." He could understand that. If

someone had come along and told him Lizzie would have him . . . Well, he'd have been knocked for a loop.

He hadn't given up on Lizzie, of course. He was not a man to give up easily. But first he had to take care of his sister.

Mitchell was beginning to get his color back, but he was still staring at the packet of powder.

"Better put that away," Worthington said. "You don't want her to see it."

"No, no. Of course not. I — must I begin immediately, milord?"

"As soon as possible. That gypsy fellow, you know."

"Yes."

Poor Mitchell. He looked like someone at Gentleman Jackson's boxing establishment had dealt him a hard left to the breadbasket.

Across London, in Elizabeth's drawing room, Caroline scooped up the little dog and scratched behind his ears. "Lizzie, I can't believe you've managed this!"

Elizabeth sighed. "It's still not settled, you know. Mitchell may refuse." She patted her friend's hand. "After all, you're not sure of his feelings."

Caroline flushed. "Of course I am sure. I know how he looks at me. I *know* he cares."

"I hope so. For if he doesn't, there is nothing more we can do."

"Oh Lizzie, our plan must work. I know I can be very happy with him."

"I'm sure you can," Elizabeth replied. "But remember, if Mitchell does agree, you must pout and be loath to give up your gypsy."

Caroline giggled. "Oh, I shall do a marvelous job. I am very good at pouting."

"No doubt Worthington will command you —"

Caroline bounced to her feet and handed the dog to his mistress. "Oh Lizzie, it is so wonderful. I cannot thank you enough!"

"I don't need thanks. Just don't let your brother know anything about this. Even after you're married."

"We won't. I promise." Caroline glanced at the clock. "Do you think I can go home now?"

"Yes, but remember, don't give in too soon."

Caroline nodded. "Oh, my goodness. I almost forgot. When is Monsieur Rience arriving?"

"Monday next, I believe. Caroline, do be careful. Your brother is no fool."

With a smile, Caroline tied the strings of her bonnet under her chin. "I know. I'll be careful. But oh, it's the most marvelous thing. I'm actually going to get married to the man I love!"

And off she went, humming a gypsy song under her breath.

Elizabeth sighed. For a moment there, she had considered giving Caroline some of Madame Nuranova's powder. This being in love was addling her wits!

And yet maybe the powder worked. If it did, and she could give some to Worthington —

This was utterly ridiculous. One did not win a husband by dropping love powder in his tea!

Chapter Twelve

It was two more days before Elizabeth saw Caroline again. She showed up at the museum with her brother and immediately went strolling off.

Elizabeth turned to Worthington. "What has happened?" she asked.

Worthington frowned. "I broached the subject to Mitchell. It was no easy task, I can tell you."

Two days she'd been waiting to hear and he had to delay like this! "What happened?" she repeated as reasonably as she could.

"He said he'd do it."

"And have you spoken to Caroline yet?"

"Not yet. It was the most curious thing. Mitchell said he had already formed an affection for her."

Slowly, carefully, Elizabeth swallowed a sigh. "So, now we have only to persuade Caroline."

"Only?" He raised a dark eyebrow. "The chit is off now, after that gypsy fellow."

"Don't worry. We'll manage."

"I hope so. Caroline can be quite stubborn."

So could he, Elizabeth thought, but of course she did not say so. "Yes, I know. But I think we shall prevail. When do you intend to tell her?"

"I thought I'd give Mitchell some time. He's quite a good chap. Maybe I won't have to command her. Maybe he'll win her by himself."

She gave him a smile. "That's kind of you."

He looked a little pained. "I do want her to be happy. But not with that gypsy! What if she runs off with him?"

Poor Tom-Tom. She didn't like seeing him in such distress. "I don't think she would do anything without telling me. And besides, the Giacondas have still a week to go on their engagement. I don't think they will leave till their time's up."

He clasped her hand in his, causing her heart to rise up in her throat and dance madly. "Thank you, Lizzie, for helping me with this."

She managed to untangle her tongue enough to say, "You're welcome. Caroline is my friend, too, you know. I want what's best for her. I want her to be happy."

"Will you — will you be present when I talk to her?"

"Of course." She wanted to urge him to hurry. Every day they delayed made the possibility of discovery more likely. But she didn't dare to say anymore about the subject. She didn't dare to do anything that might make him suspicious.

"I think I'll do it at the end of the week. He'll have had time to speak to her by then."

Elizabeth nodded, but she was still worried. How would Caroline respond when the man she loved declared himself? Would she remember to pout and refuse him? This must not look too easy.

Elizabeth was still worrying when she and Worthington entered his drawing room at the end of the week. He motioned her to a chair and sent for Mitchell.

Elizabeth tried to calm her nerves, no simple task. If this meeting went awry, if Caroline forgot her part — she couldn't bear to think of what might happen.

Mitchell came hurrying in, looking like a man who had a chance at heaven but wasn't sure he was going to make it. "Yes, milord?"

"Sit down. We'd like a report on your progress with Caroline."

The steward perched on the very edge of his chair. "I — I don't know if I've made any progress. She — she seems to like me, but —"

"You have not asked the question."

Mitchell looked startled. "Of course not, milord. It's too soon. It hasn't even been a whole week."

Worthington frowned. "I know that, man! But the gypsies are finishing up their engagement. They're going to be leaving. And Caroline can't go with them."

"Of course not. But milord —"

These two seemed determined to bungle the thing. Elizabeth leaned forward. "May I suggest something?"

"Of course."

"Why not tell Caroline that Mr. Mitchell has asked for her hand? That he knows it's very soon . . . but he has loved her for a long time. And he grows impatient."

Worthington smiled. "I like that. It has a romantic sound."

"But will Lady Caroline like it?" Mitchell asked in distress.

Worthington's expression was grim. "She is going to marry you one way or another."

"But milord, if she doesn't love me —"

"Do you want her to run off with the gypsy, then?"

Mitchell blanched. "God, no! If I lose her

now, I should — I don't know what I'd do."

Elizabeth took pity on the man. "Then let us proceed as I suggested."

Worthington nodded. "I'll send for her."

While they waited, Elizabeth watched the men. Fortunately, they were both too nervous to recognize that she, too, was on edge. So much depended on Caroline's not giving anything away.

She came into the room with a feigned look of innocence. "Why, Lizzie, how nice to see you."

Elizabeth nodded. "Caroline, please sit down."

Looking suitably curious, Caroline sat.

Both Mitchell and Elizabeth looked at Worthington. "I — ah — have something to tell you."

Caroline clapped her hands. "We're going on another journey to the gypsy camp. How thrilling!"

Worthington's frown was visible only for a moment before he managed to smooth it out. "No, that is not it. Someone, someone has asked me for your hand in marriage."

Elizabeth held her breath. Oh, please, let Caroline do it right.

"Worthington," Caroline sent her brother a look of pure disdain. "I told you. I don't wish to marry until I meet a man who makes my heart sing."

"You make *my* heart sing," Mitchell declared earnestly.

For the barest moment Elizabeth saw the pure joy on Caroline's face. Then she masked it. "Why, that's very kind of you, Mr. Mitchell. But I don't think that's what my brother has in mind."

Mitchell looked deflated and Elizabeth hastened to say, "I'm afraid you're mistaken, my dear. Your brother has given Mr. Mitchell permission to court you."

"He has?" This time Caroline managed to keep her face expressionless. "Well, I suppose anyone may *court* me."

Worthington opened his mouth, but Elizabeth stopped him by getting to her feet. "Perhaps you will walk with me to the window, Worthington. Give these two a little chance to talk."

Worthington offered her his arm immediately. As they moved off she heard Mitchell saying, "I know this is sudden. But I have loved you . . ."

Worthington stopped by the window. "What do you think?" he whispered.

Elizabeth managed a shrug. "Well, she did not refuse him outright. Perhaps he will be able to sway her. That was certainly a romantic declaration he made."

Worthington grinned. "He's such a quiet fellow. I didn't dream he had it in him."

"People," she said, carefully avoiding his eyes, "are not always what they seem."

So the days passed. Monsieur Rience arrived and the Giacondas departed — without Caroline. Despite Mitchell's persistent devotion, she pouted and proclaimed her entire indifference to him till one afternoon in early October when Worthington, with Elizabeth beside him, called his sister and his steward into the library.

In response to her brother's questions about her feelings, Caroline shrugged indifferently. She did such a good job that Worthington lost his temper. "You will marry him," he thundered down at her. "Because I say so!"

To the surprise of all, Mitchell got to his feet and put his body between Caroline and her brother. "No, milord," he said, his face going white. "We will not marry unless Lady Caroline wishes it."

Caroline looked to Elizabeth, dismay on her face. The poor girl didn't know what to do.

Mitchell turned to her. "I had hoped you

might learn to love me. But I see that you cannot. I know you value love in marriage. So — I will leave your brother's employ. I will leave London."

"You can't do that!" Worthington couldn't believe his ears — the fellow couldn't bolt after all the plans he'd made. "Not just like that. Come, come. Sit down. We'll have a cup of tea. Yes, tea, that's just the thing."

He knew Lizzie was staring at him. "Ah, I'll ring for it. And in the meantime, I wonder if I could have a word with you, Mitchell."

Mitchell followed him to the window. "I'm sorry milord, but I can't marry her unless she loves me."

"Have you used it?"

"Used what?"

"The powder, man!" He kept his voice low. "Have you used the love powder?"

"No, milord. It didn't seem the gentlemanly thing to do."

"For heaven's sake! Do you want her to love you or not?"

"Of course I do!"

"Then use it. And forget all this noble sacrifice rot and this thing about leaving London."

Mitchell smiled weakly. "I thought perhaps that would move her."

"Well, let's try the powder. You do have it with you?"

"Yes."

"Good. I'll take Lizzie out of here. Remember, Caroline has to see *you* after she drinks it."

"Yes, I know."

Minutes later Worthington and Lizzie were strolling in the garden. "What do you think?" he asked. "Will she let him go?"

"I hope not."

"I didn't expect him to be so noble."

Lizzie smiled. "He's a good man. And he loves her very much."

"Yes," he said. "I'm quite sure of that." He patted her hand. "You know, Lizzie, you were right about this. They suit each other perfectly. How did you know?"

"I know Caroline," she said, glancing at the French doors. "I know what will make her happy. At least, I — Oh look! Here they come."

Worthington looked. Caroline was leaning on Mitchell's arm, smiling up at him. As the two approached, Worthington looked from one to the other.

Mitchell smiled. "Milord, Lady Caroline has consented to be my wife."

Lizzie rushed to her. "My dear, how wonderful!"

Caroline smiled. "Yes, it is." She turned to her brother. "It was the strangest thing. When Mr. Mitchell said he meant to leave London, I knew. Quite suddenly I knew that he makes my heart sing."

Mitchell was beaming inanely. The man was obviously overcome by his good fortune.

"How soon do you wish the announcement made?" Worthington asked. "And the banns called?"

"Soon," said Caroline. "Oh, very soon." And off she sauntered on the arm of a man that a few days before had meant nothing to her. Women were the most peculiar creatures. But usually they did not make such drastic changes in the placement of their affections.

He swallowed an exclamation. Great galloping cannonballs! It was the gypsy powder. Mitchell had used the powder, and Caroline had actually come to love him!

The next day, as was his custom, Worthington arrived at the museum at closing time. Usually he took a look around, then he drove Lizzie home. Often he left her at her door, but this time when the barouche came to a halt, he said, "Do you suppose you could spare a cup of tea? I am really quite thirsty."

A curious look crossed her face, but then it was gone. "Yes," she said, "of course. Come in."

They settled in the study, strangely empty-looking, now that everything had been taken to the museum. Worthington glanced around. "Where is your defender?"

Lizzie smiled. "Nanny probably has him shut up somewhere. He got into her knitting and made a dreadful mess."

"I see." He took a seat near the tea table. While Lizzie rang for the butler and ordered tea, Worthington tried to decide how best to introduce the powder into her cup. He would have to distract her, get her to look elsewhere, and then —

Before he went to war, he had been quite a man about town, romanced several women, and he could not remember ever having felt nervous. But now . . . The powder had to work. He had to get Lizzie to care for him. She was driving him to distraction, always there — always unreachable.

She was eyeing him strangely. "Worthington, what is it? You look positively ill. Is your shoulder acting up again?"

"No, no. I'm fine."

202

"Is something wrong with Caroline?"

"No, no. The lovebirds are busy composing a piece for the *Times*."

"Then what is it?"

"I — I want to thank you again for helping me."

"I told you — it was nothing."

He shook his head. "It was *everything*."

The butler entered then with the tea, and she busied herself pouring it. Worthington watched, his thoughts in turmoil. She was so beautiful, the most beautiful woman in the world! And he wanted, actually wanted, to marry her.

"Here you are," she said, handing him a cup.

"Thank you. Ah, Lizzie, I'd like to ask another favor."

"Of course."

"I'd like to borrow that work of Mr. Shelley's. The one Caroline is always talking about."

She stared at him. "But you disagree with his philosophies."

Confound it, why hadn't he named some other writer? "Perhaps. But I should still like to read what he has to say."

"Of course." She put the teacup on the table and got to her feet. "I believe it's over here."

Her back was turned! Quickly he opened his snuffbox and added a pinch of the powder to her cup.

He was still closing the box when she turned around, but of course snuff meant nothing to her.

"Here it is. You may keep it as long as you like."

"Thank you."

She sat down. She picked up her cup. She sipped. He wished he had been there to see Caroline's transformation. What signs should he look for?

Lizzie's face was flushed, her eyes bright. She was so beautiful.

"Worthington," she said, startling him so that he almost dropped his cup.

"Yes, what is it?"

"Why are you staring at me so?"

"Excuse me. I — I was thinking of something else."

Elizabeth closed her mouth with a snap. The nerve of the man! Madame Nuranova must have been wrong. There was plenty of the powder in his tea. She had ordered it put there with the tea itself — a special brew, she'd told the servants, to be served the next time Worthington called. He had already drunk a whole cupful, and there he sat, not even thinking about her. This was all wrong.

The powder would never work. And Worthington would never kiss her again.

A tear rose to her eye, and it was followed by more. When she was unsuccessful in blinking them back, he stared at her in obvious alarm. "Lizzie, whatever is wrong?"

"I — I was just thinking of Papa. He would be so proud of the museum."

He put down his cup and got to his feet. "Come now, Lizzie. I rather think he knows all about it."

"You do?"

He came to stand in front of her. "Yes, I do."

He pulled her to her feet. He was so close, so strong. If only —

"Oh, Tom-Tom," she wailed. "I miss him so much!"

And then she let the tears flow. For a minute she sobbed there in front of him. All in vain, she thought, it was all in vain.

And then he was gathering her against his brocaded waistcoat and muttering, "There, there, don't cry."

She cried as long and as hard as she could, not an easy task when she was close against his chest, his arms around her. But finally she could call up no more tears, finally there was no more reason she could expect comfort.

Slowly he put her from him, but he was still very close, so close. She resisted the urge to burrow back into his arms, to declare her feelings for him.

His eyes were warm as he looked down at her, his expression tender. "There now, Lizzie, my dear. It will be all right. Trust me."

Trust him! If only he knew! She wanted to trust him with her life, her happiness — her love.

For a long long moment she looked up into his face. She loved him so much! How could he not know it?

"I — I don't know what came over me. I don't usually cry much."

His expression grew more tender. He inclined his head toward her. His lips came closer and closer. "Lizzie, I —"

And then the dog burst into the room and threw himself at his booted ankle.

"Thunderation!" Worthington cried, kicking his leg free. "That animal is vicious. I can't understand why you keep him."

She scooped up the snarling dog. The magic moment was gone. "Neither do I," she said quietly. "But I suppose it's because I love him."

He looked embarrassed. "Well, I'll — I'll have to be going. I'll see you tomorrow."

She watched him leave, hope growing in her breast. He had been warm. He had been tender. He had been going to kiss her. She felt it in her very bones. The powder *was* working!

She looked down at the squirming dog. "Next time he comes over, *you* are going to get some tea."

Chapter Thirteen

By Saturday Elizabeth had lost the good feeling caused by the success of her plan for Caroline. Though she tried to keep up her spirits, tried to remember that moment when Worthington had been about to kiss her, sometimes she believed she had imagined the whole thing — the looks of tenderness, the warmth in his eyes, the kiss that had been about to happen.

Weren't women in love often prone to strange imaginings? What if the force of her feelings had unsettled her mind?

She went to the museum every day, more from force of habit than anything else. The people she had hired to work there were all doing their part. And Mr. Elderby, the ticket-taker, as usual did a fine job of managing things without her help.

But she was so restless. And the usual *ton* pursuits of cards and fêtes, routes and soirées, seemed utterly ridiculous. How could she sit around gossiping about Prinny's newest *friend* when all her thoughts were centered on Worthington?

So off she went to the museum, where she could at least feel that she was being useful.

She was there on Saturday afternoon, considering the display of Indian weapons from the former Colonies, when she heard a commotion behind her.

"Lookit the pig!" a child cried. "What's he got?"

She whirled in dismay. The pig was not supposed to roam about unattended. Oh Lord, no! "Toby, stop!"

Of course he didn't. She lifted her skirts and set out after the animal, who ran squealing back toward the room he considered his sanctuary.

She cornered him there — and Mr. Ware, who was trying unsuccessfully to hide a half-empty pail of gin.

"Why, milady, what you doing here?"

"The pig has my head."

Mr. Ware stared at her in obvious puzzlement. "Your noggin's looking fine."

She felt her temper rising. This man and his pig had been nothing but trouble. In fact, the whole museum had been one fiasco after another. "The pig has taken one of my shrunken heads," she told the showman. "Get it for me. Now!"

Mr. Ware hastened to obey. After considerable squealing on Toby's part and cursing on his, Mr. Ware came back, carrying the shrunken head at arm's length. "Ugly looking thing, it is. Can't imagine why he should take it."

"Neither can I." Elizabeth took the now rather damp head by the hair. It had certainly not been improved by being carried about in Toby's mouth.

"Mr. Ware, this has got to stop. Your pig cannot be allowed to run free through the museum. You must control him."

"I know, I know." Mr. Ware bobbed his head. "He snuck out on me. He's just that curious."

"I cannot —"

"Lady Elizabeth!"

Startled, she swung around. Worthington was standing in the doorway, his face a veritable thundercloud.

She hurried to him. "What is it, milord? What's wrong?"

He ignored her and addressed a steely look to the showman. "Keep the pig in this room. Or else."

Then, taking her by the arm, he started off down the hall at a pace so swift she felt more like she was being dragged than escorted.

"Worthington, what are you doing? Where are we going?"

210

"We are going to your house," he said grimly.

"But why?"

"I have something to say to you."

"But the office — one of the rooms —"

When they reached the office, he took the shrunken head from her hand and dropped it unceremoniously onto a table. Then he bundled her into her cloak and bonnet with barely concealed impatience. She had never seen him like this.

"Worthington —"

"I don't wish to speak until we have privacy."

Once in the carriage, she turned to him again, but he gave her such a withering look that she subsided without saying a word.

They reached her house and he escorted her inside, his face still a mask of grimness. As she gave Barton her cloak and bonnet, she said, "A pot of tea, please, Barton. That special brew."

"Yes, milady."

She led the way into the drawing room and settled herself in the chair by the tea table. "Now, Worthington, will you *please* tell me what is on your mind?"

He did not take a chair but began restlessly pacing, stopping on occasion to glare down at her. "How could you?" he de-

211

manded. "How could you do such a thing?"

Her temper was already frayed from her encounter with the pig and his drunken master. And this highhandedness by Worthington did nothing to help. "How could I do *what?* Make sense, man."

"You lied to me. You deceived me."

Her heart dropped down into her stomach. "I did what?"

"You knew Caroline loved Mitchell. You knew it all along. The two of you conspired together. You set out to make a fool of me."

So now he knew. And his male pride was bruised. She decided to put up a good front. "You are mistaken," she said coldly. "You asked for my help, and I gave it."

He stopped in his angry pacing and glared at her again. "You tricked me into settling on Mitchell. Oh, yes! I know all about it. It seems that after Caroline accepted the man, she told him the truth. Told him all about her friend Lizzie and how she had helped her."

Elizabeth swallowed a groan. Why had Caroline done such a foolish thing?

"He came to me, Mitchell did, to tell me the truth."

"Because he's an honorable man," she said softly.

"What has that to do with anything?"

"I believe you wanted such a man for your sister. Honest, generous, kind, hardworking —"

"Yes, yes." He scowled. "I know all that."

"And isn't James Mitchell all of these things?"

"Yes, but that is not the point."

How could he be so stubbornly blind? "The point is that your sister is marrying a good man, a man she loves, a man who loves her."

He did not appear the least bit mollified, but continued to stamp back and forth across the Persian carpet.

"The point," he thundered, "is that I trusted you and you betrayed me!"

His words hurt, hurt so much that for a moment she did not know how to defend herself. And then another thought struck her. In his rage he might have . . .

"Did you withdraw your permission?"

If anything, he scowled more ferociously. "No. I could not do so without hurting Mitchell. And *his* behavior has been above reproach."

"Quite so," she said with a sigh of relief. "And so should Caroline's have been, had she believed you less of a tyrant."

His face turned so scarlet that for a moment she thought he might explode.

"I?" he thundered. "I, a tyrant?"

"Yes. You wished her to marry Vidon. Tell me, if she had asked to wed Mitchell then, would you have given her permission?"

"Of course —" He hesitated. "You know I would not."

"See? Then how else were we to convince you?" She tried a conciliating little smile. "Be reasonable. All has turned out well. You have lost nothing."

For a moment she thought he understood, that he would smile and become his old self. But the frown did not leave his face.

"You are mistaken," he said, his tone icy. "I have lost something quite valuable. I have lost a friend, a friend I could trust."

Why must he make things so difficult? She had not done anything so terribly outrageous.

Barton appeared in the doorway. "The tea, milady."

Worthington smiled sardonically. "Serve her ladyship," he said, and marched out.

Elizabeth bit back an exclamation. The foolish man couldn't mean what he'd said. Why, he made it sound as though their friendship were over, as though she would never see him again. Such thoughts sent her heart into a frenzied beating.

No, that could not happen. This would blow over, just like their other tiffs. It had to.

But three days passed without a sign of Worthington or his sister. Elizabeth was too nervous to try calling on them. And besides, she found events at the museum taking a turn for the worse. Toby's occasional forays into the gin pail had become a daily, ever growing, indulgence.

She had put it off, hoping Worthington would come around and she could ask him to do it. But by the middle of the week she knew she could not wait. So she took herself back to the room that Toby occupied.

The two of them, pig and master, were lolling in the straw. Mr. Ware jumped hastily to his feet. The pig merely grunted.

"You have had a long engagement, Mr. Ware. I believe most of London has seen Toby perform."

"Yeah, yer ladyship." Mr. Ware grinned foolishly. "Toby, he's become real famous."

Elizabeth nodded. "Yes. Well, your engagement will be finished at the end of next week."

Mr. Ware turned white. "It will?"

"Yes. I suggest you take Toby home. I

think he misses the country."

"I don't know about him, milady. I know I do miss it. But you're sure you won't be needing us?"

"I'm sure," Elizabeth said. "Thank you for your services."

She left quickly then, before Mr. Ware could beg for an extension on their engagement. The sooner he left the fleshpots, or more accurately the ginpots, of the city, the better off he would be.

Now what was she to do? Monsieur Rience was still drawing people, but the London crowds were fickle. Soon they would be tired of him.

Toby had been the best attraction of all. And, contrary to what she had just told his master, he was still drawing crowds. But the pig had already caused one riot and nearly started another. A drunken man was bad enough, but 600 pounds of drunken pig was too much.

She opened her ink bottle and picked up a quill. Perhaps Madame Nuranova could find her another learned animal, one less disposed to gin pails than Toby.

On Wednesday morning Worthington left the present abode of the Little Dove — and he was wearing a frown. Life had become extremely complicated of late. Things that had once been the best part of his life — a fine horse, a good mill, an exciting game of cards, a willing bit of muslin — all had lost their ability to please him.

He had just assured the Little Dove that he had no complaints about her behavior. The fault lay in him. That apology and a good settlement had made the parting more amicable than most, but it still sat uneasily upon him.

Who would ever have imagined that he would voluntarily give up one of London's best ladies of the night? And that because of a woman who had treated him as abominably as Lizzie had.

It was clever, though, that scheme of hers. So clever that he had not suspected a thing. He smiled. Lizzie was intelligent, all right. And she understood Caroline. He sighed. If she only understood *him* half as well.

Still, he had let her stew long enough. She should be thoroughly chastened by now. Perhaps she would even be willing to listen to him for a change. He turned the barouche toward the museum.

Mr. Elderby pulled at his sparse side hair. "She ain't here, milord. Ain't been here all day."

It wasn't like Lizzie to stay home. "Is she ill?"

The ticket taker shook his head. "Oh no, milord. She's gone."

Worthington swallowed an exclamation. "Gone where?"

"I don't rightly know, milord. 'Cepting it's someplace in Surrey. Said we was gonna get a horse what could count."

"A horse? But what of Toby?"

"He's gone, milord. Mr. Ware, too." Mr. Elderby wrinkled his rather large nose. "And good riddance, I says. Why, that pig, he was drunk most every night. And that master of his, too. Her ladyship just had to let 'em go."

"Of course." Worthington tried to think. "Mr. Elderby, do you know anything more, anything that might help me find her?"

"Well now, let me think. There was a fellow, gypsy fellow, he brought the message 'bout the horse. He said —" He scratched his head. "I think he said he was staying at the Inn of the Green Knight. Something about playing his violin."

Worthington swallowed a curse. "Thank you, Mr. Elderby. You've been most helpful."

Worthington turned back to the carriage. Lizzie had left the city without telling him.

How could she . . .

He knew very well how — she had thought their friendship finished. All because he had let the Worthington temper control his tongue. He tried to remember what he had said to her. Something about losing a trusted friend.

He'd been very harsh. And that after she had indicated that his friendship meant so much to her.

Stupid fool! His curse startled the horses and caused several passersby to stare at him in surprise.

It was his fault Lizzie was traveling about with only Nanny and Elias to protect her. She had believed their friendship over. That's why she hadn't notified him about the trip.

Well, he would find this gypsy if it took all afternoon. And as soon as he got the necessary information he would be on the road. Lizzie was out there somewhere. And he meant to be with her.

After several fruitless hours of searching, he returned home to find a package had been delivered during his absence. "A gypsy left it," the butler reported, a slight curl to his lip. "I didn't want to take it, but he insisted it was something you had requested.

Said you could make payment at the Knight's Head Inn. He said you knew him."

That was it! The Knight's Head, not Head of the Green Knight.

Worthington grabbed the package. "I may be gone a day or two," he said. "Tell my sister not to worry. I have gone after Lady Elizabeth."

Chapter Fourteen

When Worthington sighted Lizzie's carriage late that afternoon, he still had no idea what he would say to her. But when he recognized the Farrington crest, he put the spurs to the stallion and raced onward. He could think only of seeing Lizzie's dear face.

Her equipage was just entering a patch of dark woods and he yelled to the coachman to wait up. But the fool looked back over his shoulder and then whipped up the horses. "Stop!" Worthington shouted. "Don't run the horses in there!"

But the driver either could not, or would not, hear, and the carriage went barreling off at a horrendous pace.

Lizzie was in that carriage! What could Elias be thinking of? Worthington bent low, urging the horse on. And then, to his complete surprise, he heard a pistol report and the familiar whine of a bullet whizzing by his head. Good lord! Someone was shooting at him!

Automatically he pulled the stallion up. Why should Elias shoot at him? As he stared after it, the carriage rounded a bend out of sight. Moments later he heard a resounding crash, followed by the neighing of hysterical horses.

"Lizzie! My God!" Once more he spurred the stallion forward. "Lizzie!"

He rounded the bend at a full gallop and had to haul the stallion to a skidding halt. Off to one side of the road, the carriage leaned drunkenly against a tree, one wheel gone. At least it was still upright. "Lizzie," he called, hastily swinging down. "Are you all right?"

"Worthington? Is that you?" Her voice was shaky, but it was music to his ears.

"Yes, it's me."

Her face appeared in the carriage window, pale but with no marks on it. "I cannot open the door," she said. "It seems to be jammed."

He hastened forward and gave it a good hard pull. When the door came off in his hand, he tossed it aside. "Are you injured?"

She stared at him. "No. I think not."

He reached up. "Let me help you down."

"Thank you."

He lifted her down. "Are you sure you're all right?"

He could feel the trembling of her body, but she nodded. "I'm fine. But please, do see to Nanny."

"Of course." Reluctantly he released her and turned to the carriage. Thrusting his head inside, he saw that Nanny lay unconscious. Carefully he lifted her out. "It looks like she's got a bump on her head. But I think she'll be all right."

Nanny moaned and opened her eyes. "Merciful heavens!" she cried, looking up into his face. "Put me down this very instant!"

Worthington complied. Nanny was no lightweight. Still, with that knot on her head . . . "Be careful now, you've got a nasty lump there."

Nanny shivered. "I'm just that glad we got away." She looked to Lizzie. "Did you tell him?"

"Tell me what?" he inquired.

"A highwayman was after us," Lizzie said.

"And she shot at him. She was that brave."

Worthington sighed. "She was that foolish."

Lizzie stared at him, her foot starting to tap. "Foolish?"

"Yes. I'm afraid you shot at me."

"At you! But Elias said —"

"I suspect Elias does not see so well. You shot at me. The bullet went right past my head."

She paled slightly, but then she straightened and gave a forced laugh. "I am usually a better shot."

My word! She meant to laugh at this! "You should not be shooting at all," he said sternly. "And why did you leave London without telling me?"

A little color came back into her cheeks. "I did not think you wished to accompany me any longer."

He scowled. "Don't be foolish. I gave you my word. I intend to keep it."

Obviously she didn't know how to respond to that. And while she stood there thinking, Nanny cried, "Look! There's Elias."

The coachman was lying a few feet away, the reins still wrapped around his hand. The horses, dragging the broken carriage shaft, now grazed peacefully nearby.

"Oh dear!" Lizzie ran to kneel at his side. "*Elias!* Oh please, speak to me!"

The coachman's eyes fluttered open. He stared, then started to sit up. "The horses —"

"Lie still," Lizzie ordered. "The horses are fine. We are all fine. You did an excellent job."

Elias glanced around. "That highwayman — where'd he go?"

Lizzie had the grace to look embarrassed. "Ah, Elias, it wasn't a highwayman. It was Worthington."

Elias turned first purple and then white. "You — you fired at his lordship?"

"Yes." Elizabeth had never felt so embarrassed.

Worthington chuckled. "She's a poor shot. Missed me by a mile."

The nerve of the man — and just when she'd been so happy to see him. But why must the two of them keep refining on the thing? Of course she hadn't hit him. She'd aimed high on purpose.

"Perhaps," she said, casting an acid glance at Worthington, "we should do something besides discuss my marksmanship. Nanny has a lump on her head. And you, Elias, have you been hurt?"

"I ain't sure. Just let me feel bones."

To her relief his examination revealed no injuries. He got slowly to his feet. "I'll just tie these here horses and see about the carriage."

"It's no use," Worthington told him. "When you lost the wheel, the axle cracked."

Elias groaned. "She'll need repairing then."

Worthington nodded. "So, I suggest we

make for the nearest town. Which is?"

"Bath," Elizabeth replied. "But how shall we get there?"

Worthington smiled, and in spite of her irritation she felt a surge of joy. She really was glad to see him.

"We have two choices," he said. "Shanks mare, or —"

"I ain't walking," Nanny declared brusquely. "Nary a step I ain't."

"Or you can ride one of the horses," Worthington continued.

"Ride?" Nanny's voice shot up into a screech that set the horses to prancing skittishly. "I ain't never been on a horse in my life. And I ain't about to start now."

Worthington shrugged. "Well, then, you'd best find yourself a nice spot under a tree. We'll send someone back for you."

And while Nanny stared at him, he turned. "Come, Lizzie, you can ride behind me and Elias can bring the carriage horses."

"I —" Elizabeth saw immediately that it was pointless to protest. Certainly she could not walk to Bath. And in her present unsettled condition, she did not have the strength — or the inclination — to ride the restive stallion alone.

Worthington swung up and offered her his hand. "Elias, help her up."

With the coachman's assistance, she was soon perched behind the saddle. "He's a little fidgety," Worthington said. "Not used to carrying double. So hang on tight."

"Yes, of course." She put her arms around his waist. Her heart was pounding so crazily. Surely he must be able to feel it against his back!

She rested her head against his broad shoulder. The faint scent of clean linen and pomade made her lightheaded. Or was that because she was so close to him?

"All set?" he asked.

"Yes." She managed to get the word out.

"Then —"

"Wait! You can't leave me here." Nanny scowled up at them. "It ain't decent."

Elizabeth sighed. She was too exhausted to deal with the old woman now, but she must. After all, Nanny was her responsibility.

And then Worthington said, "Decency has nothing to do with it, Nanny. We have only the choices I mentioned. You may walk along with us, ride one of the carriage horses, or wait."

Nanny snorted. "I suppose I'll have to walk, then," she said grimly. "And me an old woman."

Elias coughed apologetically. "I could be

staying, too, milord, if you so like."

Elizabeth swallowed hastily. If they were alone, would Worthington kiss —

"No, we can't do that," Nanny said, though it was obvious she was tempted. "There's her reputation to think of. If someone was to see them together, and me not there —"

Elizabeth felt the sigh that shivered over Worthington's entire body. But what did it mean?

Then he said, "We shall have to get started, then."

They reached the inn about an hour later. Elizabeth, sliding down into Worthington's hands, was sorry the ride was over. Even Nanny's constant complaints couldn't dampen the joy of being so close to him. Now she stood, staring up into the face she loved, wishing . . . But even if he wanted to, he could do nothing while the others were there.

"I'll get you a room," he said, smiling down at her. "Then I'll see about getting the carriage fixed."

"Thank you. And — thank you for coming after me."

"You're welcome." His eyes darkened. "Lizzie, listen. I'm sorry about what I said to you that day. I was distraught."

She felt the tears rising to her eyes, but she couldn't cry now. "I thought — it seemed that our friendship was over. I truly didn't think you would want to come with me."

"I should want —"

"Ohhhh!" Nanny groaned. "Where is that room? I need a place to lay my aching bones. And my poor head's a-pounding fiercer than ever."

"Of course," Worthington said courteously. "Come, I'll help you in."

Soon he had them settled. "I'll be back to tell you about the carriage. Of course we'll have to spend the night here. It's too late to get anything fixed now."

Nanny sighed. "I don't care, long as I've got a decent bed."

He smiled and was gone, leaving Elizabeth to settle Nanny down and wonder what it was he'd been about to say when the old nurse had interrupted him.

It was several hours before his tapping on the door announced his return. "Have you eaten?" he asked.

She shook her head. "No, Nanny went right off to sleep. And I did not think it wise to go downstairs alone."

He nodded. "Of course not. But you must eat. Come, join me now."

She glanced at the sleeping Nanny. "I should like to. But if someone should see us, and Nanny not present — after all, she walked all that way because of me. And you know how people talk."

He smiled. "Ah yes. The tongues would wag. And far more than they have over your museum."

"Yes." She was glad he could see what she meant, but she was also disappointed.

"But I cannot have you eating alone." He glanced around. "I know, I shall have a supper sent up here. And I shall join you."

She wanted that very much. "But — but Nanny is sleeping."

He grinned. "So she is. But I won't tell anyone if you won't."

And so they settled down to quite an acceptable supper. The beef was a little stringy and the tea a trifle weak, but to Elizabeth it was heavenly. Worthington was talking to her. He was still her friend.

"Tell me about the learned horse," he said, wiping his mouth with his napkin. "Mr. Elderby said you had to let Toby go."

"Yes. It was sad. But the pig was drinking every night. And after he stole the shrunken head —" She paused, remembering the pain of that day. "Well, he just got worse and worse. So I had to let him go."

Worthington nodded. "I see that. But Lizzie, a horse?"

"He can do all that Toby could do." Why must he look at her like that? "Madame Nuranova wrote that she saw him perform herself."

"Perhaps. But he cannot live in that room."

"I know that. He can be stabled in the mews behind the museum."

"But where is he to perform?"

"In the main room, of course."

"Lizzie, this is a museum you have, not Ashley's Amphitheatre. We're talking about a *horse*. To the best of my knowledge, a horse cannot be housebroken."

"I —" He was right. What could she have been thinking? The truth was she had not considered all the ramifications of engaging the horse. And that was because she was so upset over him. She had not been able to think straight since he'd stomped out of her life. "Perhaps you're right," she said finally. "I'll think on it."

He heaved a sigh of relief. "So you haven't engaged the horse yet?"

"No. We didn't travel as fast as you."

He frowned. "I was worried about you.

Alone like that."

"There was no need. I had protection."

He grimaced. "A pistol! A pistol you almost killed me with!"

The thought took her breath away, but she refused to feel faint. "I did not aim to hit. I wanted to scare the highwayman off."

His mouth twisted into a grin. "Well, you certainly succeeded. I'm sure any bona fide highwayman would have turned tail and run."

She felt the blood rushing to her face. "Really, Worthington, I am sorry. Elias said a highwayman was following us. And so naturally I got out my pistol."

"Naturally." He shook his head. "And who taught you to fire a pistol?"

"Papa, of course. He wanted me to be safe."

Worthington nodded. "Well, thank goodness you aimed to miss."

"Yes. Thank goodness." To think that she might have shot him! She was overwhelmed with such a rush of tenderness that if the table had not been between them, she might have thrown herself against his waistcoat. Instead, she managed a little laugh. "I should have missed our arguments quite dreadfully."

He laughed, too, but something changed

in his eyes. "We are not arguing now," he said softly.

"No, we are not. But — but no doubt we shall begin again."

"Perhaps."

His gaze held hers until a soft snore from Nanny broke the silence. He glanced at his timepiece, then at the night sky outside the window. "I suppose I should leave you to your rest. We'll probably be able to start for home shortly after noon tomorrow."

She nodded. "We'll be ready." She wanted him to stay, to talk to her as he had been doing, to . . .

He got to his feet and looked down at the table. "I'll send someone up to take care of this."

"Yes." She followed him to the door, stood there while he opened it, her heart thumping madly. If he meant to kiss her, now was the time. He gazed down at her, looking so handsome, while her knees slowly turned to jelly.

"Till tomorrow," he said, bending toward her.

She closed her eyes and raised her face eagerly for his kiss. But his lips did not meet hers. Instead they brushed her forehead in the briefest caress. "Goodnight."

She opened her eyes quickly, but he was

already half out the door. Slowly she shut it behind him. Well, she'd gotten her wish. They were friends. A sob caught in her throat. Only friends.

Outside the door, Worthington smiled sadly. This time he had managed to do the gentlemanly thing. Lizzie would surely appreciate his restraint. Too bad she would never know what it had cost him.

Chapter Fifteen

The next morning found Elizabeth bleary-eyed and weary. All night she had lain awake, going over what had happened between them. Her heart had pounded and her cheeks grown hot as she relived those last moments by the door. But always she came back to the same unsatisfying conclusion. What Worthington felt for her was brotherly affection, nothing more.

Of course, what she felt for him was something else altogether. She shed more than a few tears, but finally, toward morning, she dried her eyes. And there in the darkness she had made herself a solemn promise. She would not give up. After all, they were friends again. They would be spending time together. Therefore there was hope.

So near noon when he came knocking at the door, she went to open it with a smile. "The carriage is ready," he said. "You may send Nanny on down. But could you stop with me for a moment? I left something in my room that I want to show you."

"Of course." She turned back to the nurse. "We'll be down in a minute."

"Very well." Nanny sniffed. "But no more than a minute."

Elizabeth sighed. It was time Nanny stopped treating her like a child, but this was not the place to discuss it.

Worthington's room was just four doors down the hall. Elizabeth stepped inside while he went to retrieve a parcel that lay on the table across the room.

"What —" she began.

And then from the hallway came a gasp — and a terrible giggle. "See, Mama? I told you! It *was* them!"

Elizabeth turned. It couldn't be, but it was. Miss Linden stood in the hallway. And beside her loomed the bulk of her formidable mama.

"I never would have believed it," Lady Linden said with obvious glee, "if I hadn't seen it with my own eyes."

The blood rushed to Elizabeth's cheeks. The Lindens believed she had shared this room with Worthington. "Wait," she cried. "You are mistaken!"

But Miss Linden elevated her thin nose and marched off behind her mama.

The room began to spin and Elizabeth put a hand to her forehead. What were those abominable Lindens doing so far from London?

"Lizzie? Lizzie, are you ill?"

Finally she realized that Worthington was speaking to her. He looked so ordinary, standing there. "Didn't you see? The Lindens! They saw me here in your room. Now they think —"

He stared at her. "Think what?"

"They think that you and I — that we —" She couldn't finish.

He raised an eyebrow. "Oh Lizzie, come on now. Nanny is waiting out in the carriage."

"That doesn't signify. The Lindens saw me in your room. By nightfall all London will know about it. My reputation will be ruined."

Worthington stared at her. He couldn't believe that sane sensible Lizzie was carrying on so — and over a couple of known gossip-mongers like the Lindens. "You're refining too much on the matter," he said.

And then, incredibly, right in front of him, she burst into tears. He stared at her for a moment while she sobbed with heartbroken abandon. Then he did the only thing he could think to do. He gathered her into his arms.

She sobbed there for some minutes while

he gave himself over to the thought that he would like to hold her thus forever.

Finally she straightened and pulled back. "I'm — I'm sorry. I cannot imagine why I behaved so foolishly. The Lindens are terrible liars, of course. But still some people will believe them." She sighed. "I shall live it down, though. Just as I lived down the gossip about the museum."

Her lower lip quivered so he longed to kiss it steady. And then it came to him: here was the opportunity he'd been looking for! "It's all right, Lizzie. Listen, I know how to fix it. You and I, we'll get married. They won't talk about you then."

Her face changed expression several times, but they were never expressions he could read. Once he thought she swayed slightly toward him, but then she straightened, said, "Don't be foolish, Worthington," and swept past him out the door.

He picked up the parcel and hurried after her. He certainly hadn't expected a reaction like that. Foolish, indeed!

When he reached the courtyard Elias was helping her into the carriage. Worthington looked around, but there was no sign of the ubiquitous Lindens. He stopped by the carriage window. "We'll discuss the matter some more when we reach London."

She shook her head. "No, we won't."

Turning away, he mounted the stallion. The vagaries of the female mind were more than he could fathom. But they would discuss it again, whether she wished to or not. Her reputation was a matter of importance, and he wasn't going to allow the Lindens to ruin it.

He frowned. They'd already ruined giving her the gift as he'd planned. He patted the parcel tied to the saddle. He would just have to present it after they reached London.

Inside the carriage Elizabeth sat silent, trying to think, trying to decide what to do. Perhaps she would leave London, go to her country estate to live. But no! She had never been one to run away, and she wouldn't do it now. She would face up to the *ton* and its whispers.

Of course, if she accepted Worthington, the whispers would soon be stilled. And she had wanted to accept him — wanted to so much that she had almost said yes right then, almost run into his arms.

But then she had seen she couldn't do it. A marriage of convenience, or of friendship, as in this case, might work if both parties were of the same mind. But if one of them were much in love — and the other knew nothing of it — disaster was imminent.

She fixed her unseeing eyes on the passing scenery. Yes, she had been tempted. But the prospect of sharing the man she loved with another woman . . . She just couldn't face it.

"Well," Nanny said sourly. "You're overquiet today."

"I'm tired," Elizabeth replied. "I did not sleep well last night."

Nanny fixed her with a shrewd eye. "And why not, I wonder? Because you're running around after strange creatures instead of looking for a hus—"

"Nanny!" The sharpness of her voice caused the old nurse to jump. "Please," Elizabeth said in a softer tone. "I have a headache and I do not wish to talk."

Nanny's eyes narrowed. "You didn't have no headache afore. What's wrong?"

Elizabeth was tempted to burst into tears and spill out the whole horrible story, but she stopped herself in time. If Nanny knew the truth, she would push for marriage. And Elizabeth didn't know if she could withstand them both. "Nothing is wrong," she insisted. "I just wish to be quiet."

They reached London in the late afternoon. As he helped her down, she avoided Worthington's eyes. If he had any idea of what she was thinking, feeling — She would

240

be mortified if he ever found out. "Thank you for your help," she said formally. "It was most kind of you."

Her formal tone had Nanny staring, and even Elias cast her a bewildered look.

"It was no trouble," Worthington said. "But I should like a cup of tea."

"I am very tired, and —" Seeing Nanny's look of surprise, she knew she would have to capitulate. "Of course, come in."

She ordered the tea and lowered herself wearily into a chair. Worthington settled into another. "Well, Nanny," he said. "What do you think we should do?"

Nanny, who had just eased herself down, stared at him. "Do about what?" she asked.

"About the Lindens."

Since he was studiously avoiding looking at Elizabeth, he did not right away see the imploring signals she was sending him. And then it was too late. Nanny turned to look at her. "What has the Lindens to do about things?"

Elizabeth saw that there would be no peace till she had faced this. "They were there, in the inn. And they saw us."

Nanny frowned. "Saw what?"

Worthington sighed. "I'm afraid they saw the two of us in my room. And they jumped to some —"

"Merciful heavens!" Nanny wailed. "I knew it. I just knew it! My baby's been ruined. It was all this gallivanting about. If it hadn't been for that crazy museum of yours, you'd have been safe at home. Oh dear, oh dear. Whatever will we do?"

"Nanny." Elizabeth knew her tone was harsh, but the old nurse was only making matters worse. "We will not *do* anything. We will go on as if nothing has happened."

Nanny stared at her. "You can't do that! Why, why, they'll keep you out of Almack's. They'll give you the cut direct. They'll —"

"Nanny, stop! I haven't gone to Almack's since the museum opened. I can certainly survive without their warm lemonade and stale cake."

"Oh dear!" Nanny began to sob into a copious white handkerchief that she extracted from her reticule.

Worthington coughed. "Come, Nanny. There's no need for tears."

" 'Tis my baby," she managed between sobs. "And she's ruined."

"Not if she marries me."

Nanny's head jerked erect, her sobs stopping instantly. "Marries you?"

"Yes. I told her it was the thing to do."

"No." Elizabeth made her tone as flat as possible. "The answer is still no."

"But milady," Nanny coaxed. "Worthington's not a bad sort. The two of you should deal famously together."

Elizabeth pushed herself wearily to her feet. "There is no point in further talk," she said. "I have said no and I mean no. Now, if you'll excuse me —"

Worthington rose. "Of course," he said. "You need some rest. I'll come back tomorrow and we'll talk some more."

"No!" She glared at them. "I am going to bed. Goodbye."

It was not till she had reached her chamber that she thought to wonder what sort of tea Barton would offer them. And then, thinking of Nanny and Worthington drinking the gypsy potion together, she fell to laughing. But her laughter turned quickly to tears. Not even gypsy magic could make Worthington love her.

The next morning she forced herself to return to her usual routine. She was about ready to leave for the museum when Barton appeared in the doorway. "Lady Caroline and Mr. James Mitchell."

Elizabeth got quickly to her feet. "Caroline, my dear. How are you?"

"I am fine. Or I will be when I apologize," Caroline said. "I did not mean to tell James about your helping us. But we were talking and it just — it just spilled out." She frowned. "He didn't tell me he was going to inform Worthington. Else I should have let you know."

Elizabeth sighed. "I think I can understand. I am glad you aren't keeping secrets from your husband-to-be."

Caroline smiled up into Mitchell's face and Elizabeth swallowed over the lump in her throat. She would never see that kind of look on Worthington's face.

James Mitchell looked at her nervously. "I wish to apologize, too, Lady Elizabeth. But his lordship has always treated me as a gentleman. And I could not do this thing behind his back."

"I understand," Elizabeth repeated. "Do not worry about it. Worthington was angry at first. But he is over that now."

"He — he seemed upset this morning," Caroline said. "Have you two had words again?"

Elizabeth managed a smile. "Not exactly. Didn't he tell you what happened?"

Caroline shook her head. "No, he only said that he cannot understand women. Whatever is going on?"

"You will learn later," Worthington said from the doorway. He looked to Elizabeth.

"You'll excuse Barton. I told him I would announce myself."

"I see." She wished she knew some way to keep her silly heart from leaping about in her breast when she saw this man. "Well, come in, then."

Worthington looked at the other two. "On your way out?"

"No," Caroline began.

But Mitchell silenced her with a look. "Yes, milord. We'll see you later, Lady Elizabeth."

"Very well." She wished she could get them to stay. She did not want Worthington to bring up marriage again. But obviously Mitchell was eager to get away.

Worthington waited till the others were gone. Then he asked, "Feeling better this morning?"

"Yes, of course. But I don't wish to —"

"I have come to give you a present." He smiled ruefully. "That was my intent at the inn — before we were so rudely interrupted."

He held out a brown paper parcel. "It is not, perhaps, the one you want. If I could, I should give you my own, in recompense for the trouble I have caused you. But since I need it right now, this will have to suffice."

She stared at the parcel he had pushed

into her hands. "Whatever are you talking about?"

His grin broadened. "Open it and see."

She sighed. "Very well. Just let me sit down." She settled on the sofa and he took a seat beside her. He was too close, but she could not move now. Slowly she untied the strings and folded back the paper. And then she stared. For a long moment she simply stared. Was this the something Madame Nuranova had seen him carrying? What did it mean, his giving her a shrunken head?

"It's not broken, is it?" he asked anxiously.

"No, no."

"You can add it to your collection."

"Thank you. But you shouldn't have —"

"I wanted to apologize for the horrible things I said to you before. I know I can trust you."

"Yes, of course," she said. "I am your friend."

He looked into her eyes. "Then why don't you trust me?"

The question shocked her. "I do. I do trust you."

"Then why won't you let me help you with this gossip thing?"

She set the head aside and got to her feet. "It's not just a question of help. I — I cannot marry *because of* the Lindens. I — I must *love* the man I marry. He must make my heart sing."

He got up and came to stand near her. "We are friends already. Perhaps you could learn to love me."

She was so tempted, tempted to tell him that that wouldn't be necessary, that already she loved him with all her heart and soul, but she knew it would not serve. "I cannot do it," she said. "I will not let the Lindens run my life."

Worthington scowled. "So you're going to let them ruin it, instead."

"I'm not," she insisted stubbornly. "I'll go everywhere and do everything I did before. The talk will die down."

"But your chances of marriage will be ruined."

"I don't wish to marry anyone." What a lie that was!

"Then you should marry me."

She stared at him. Why was he so persistent? "Worthington, you are not making sense. Why, if I don't wish to marry, should I marry you?"

"Because — because it would save you from marrying anyone else."

She felt her control slipping away. Soon she would be sobbing — or screaming. "I will not have a marriage of convenience," she cried. "Nor of friendship. Oh please, why can't you just go away and leave me alone?"

It was the last thing she wanted, but she could not stand much more of this. Oh, why couldn't he just love her?

"Very well," he said stiffly. "If that's what you wish." He turned and was at the door. And she knew she couldn't do it, she couldn't let him go. "Tom-Tom," she whispered, and then she crumpled to the floor.

He didn't get there in time to catch her, but that was all right. She had managed to do it gracefully and where there was carpet. She kept her eyes closed, her features composed. Let him think her unconscious.

Of course, it was a foolish thing she'd done. She was not the sort to swoon. And sooner or later, she would have to open her eyes. She would still have to refuse him.

"Lizzie!" he cried, gathering her up in his arms. "Oh, Lizzie, for God's sake. Why do you torture me like this? How can I tell you I love you when you behave so stubbornly?"

His lips were on her forehead or he would have seen her eyes fly open. "What — what did you say?" she mumbled.

He drew back, his face pale. "I — I wondered if you'd hurt yourself."

"No. I heard you. You said —"

"All right, I said that I love you. So laugh at me. I would have told you before, but you were so adamant. I knew you couldn't love me. And — and I have my pride."

She stared at him. "You — love — me."

"Yes. Now laugh."

"If I laugh, it will be at myself."

"Why?"

"Because I love you."

He stared at her. "What?"

"I do. Tom-Tom, *I love you.*"

He pulled her back into his arms. "What a pair of idiots we've been. Each of us nursing our pride." He kissed her nose. "Oh, Lizzie, I love you dreadfully."

"And I you." She began to giggle. "The head! That's what Madame Nuranova saw you carrying. Don't forget, my dear, you promised to invite her to our wedding."

"Oh, I shall. After all, she helped me."

She looked at him. The gypsy couldn't have . . . "Did she perhaps give you something?"

He smiled sheepishly. "Yes. A love powder. Mitchell used it on Caroline. And I — I put it in your tea."

She kissed his cheek. "Don't feel guilty, my love. I put it in your tea, too."

"You did?"

"Yes. Madame Nuranova also gave me some."

He kissed her soundly, and a very satisfying kiss it was. Then he said, "The gypsies may camp on any of our estates whenever they please. And I completely forgive you for that business over Caroline. Though it was rather underhanded."

"Yes. It was. But I am glad it came out. Husbands and wives should not keep secrets." Oh dear, she would have to tell him about that, too. "Tom-Tom, there is one more thing you should know."

He drew back a little and looked at her. "What is it? Not some freakish new thing you have in mind doing? You don't mean to build a palace to rival Prinny's Brighton Pavilion? Or open a new museum devoted only to heads?"

"Gracious, no. In fact, I think I shall leave most of the running of the museum to Mr. Elderby. I shall be quite busy being your wife."

"Then what is it?"

She took a deep breath. "Well, I — I was not exactly truthful about the museum. That is, it was not exactly Papa's dying wish. And I did not exactly promise him. But I knew that was what he would want."

Worthington frowned. "And you knew I

would accept a dying wish without a murmur. I wonder if I should marry such a conniving woman. You will be leading me around all the time."

For the space of a minute he stared at her. Her heart did all manner of strange things while she wondered if she would lose him over this final indignity.

Then he laughed and drew her against him again. "You know me so well, my love. I shall have to be very careful not to live in your pocket."

The door opened and Nanny appeared in the doorway. "Lady Elizabeth —" she began. Then she caught sight of them, there on the floor, in each other's arms, and she clapped her hands in glee. "Well, it's about time. I thought the two of you would never come to —"

"It was Madame Nuranova's love powder," Elizabeth said with a smile. "You must not malign the gypsies again."

Nanny grinned. "Them gypsies ain't half bad once you get to know them. But 'tweren't no love powder did this. Why, you've been loving this boy since you was ten years old."

Elizabeth smiled. "You know, Tom-Tom, I think she's right."

"I *know* I'm right," Nanny said. "Always have been."

Just then Fufu raced into the room, threw himself into Worthington's arms, and began to lick his face. "Well," he said. "What is this?"

Elizabeth laughed. "Fufu is an intelligent animal. He knows that you are master here now."

Worthington laughed. "I would not lay bets on it," he said, and pulled her into his arms.